# Walt Disney's *Annette*
## SIERRA SUMMER

*Authorized Edition*

**Featuring ANNETTE, star of
motion pictures and television**

## By
## Doris Schroeder

**Illustrated by
Adam Szwejkowski**

DISNEY
PRESS

NEW YORK

Printed in the United States of America

First Edition
1 3 5 7 9 10 8 6 4 2

Library of Congress Catalog Card Number on file.

ISBN 0-7868-4561-9
For more Disney Press fun, visit www.disneybooks.com

# Contents

# 1        *Vacation Bound*

"Are you sure you'll be safe, driving all that distance alone?"

It was the third time that morning that Aunt Lila had asked Annette the same question, and for the third time, Annette stopped packing to smile reassuringly at her gray-haired aunt and answer, "Of course, Auntie! Please stop worrying! I'll have a ball!"

Annette's uncle Archie had brought them with him from Ashford six months earlier, when he was sent to open a branch office of his firm in Los Angeles. Now, he and his sister Lila were leaving within a few hours for home, to close up their big house and move back to the city on the Pacific Coast permanently. And until a couple of days ago,

Annette had planned to go with them. Then a letter had come from San Francisco in her cousin Tonia's excited handwriting. It had changed her plans.

Several years before, when Annette was almost ten, her parents had taken her to visit her mother's brother, Eugenio Bori, and his family at the historic Bori home in the Sierra foothill town of Lost Creek. She had spent a happy summer with them and had never forgotten the fun that she and Tonia had shared together. Tonia, as fair as Annette was dark, was only a few months older than her cousin, and the two girls had been inseparable: two small, overalled, barefooted explorers, always into something.

They had cried on each other's shoulders when the end of summer had brought the visit to an end, and had promised solemnly to see each other the following summer.

But an accident had orphaned Annette before that time, and she had gone to live with her father's brother and sister in a distant city. She couldn't keep her promise. But she and Tonia had written each other faithfully all those years, and now, with Annette living only a couple of hundred miles away in the same state, it seemed that there was finally a chance for them to be together again.

"Do you mind very much if I go to Lost Creek instead

of helping with the move?" Annette asked as she laid aside the dainty white nylon party dress she had been carefully folding to pack in her bag. She went over and sat down on the edge of her bed beside Aunt Lila.

"Of course not, dear. As a matter of fact, if you're not around"—she smiled mischievously—"I'll have a chance to throw out a lot of those old souvenirs you've collected when I pack!"

"Aunt Lila! You wouldn't!" For a moment, Annette looked stricken. Then she saw the twinkle in her aunt's eye, and she laughed and gave her a hasty hug. "I know you're just teasing!"

"You never can tell!" Her aunt laughed with her. Then she grew more serious. "At least one member of the family will be resting! I wish I could go with you!"

Annette's big, dark eyes danced. "Tonia's letter doesn't say a word about resting!" She picked up a letter from the bedside table. "Her letter doesn't sound as if there will be much time for it! Just listen"—and she read aloud—"'We'll be down from San Francisco to open the house a week before the Pioneer Days celebration begins. So, if you get here by the twenty-eighth, you won't miss a day of it. It should be loads of fun, especially this year—the centennial! They've planned more of a thing than ever, and we'll be right in the middle of it!'"

"I can imagine," Aunt Lila said with a laugh.

Annette smiled and read on: "'The whole town is going to try to turn back the clock to the gold rush days. They'll choose a queen to ride in the parade and reign over the Square Dance Ball. And all week, there'll be tours of old mines and visits to ghost towns, and all the merchants are trying to win the Whiskerino contest prize that goes to the man with the most gorgeous beard! Dad says the prize is a free shave every week for a year!

"'And there'll be gold panning in the creeks and the biggest nugget gets a prize! Please, please, Annette, do get your aunt and uncle to bring you! Or if they can't make it, maybe they'll let you drive your new sports car. The snow is almost gone in the Sierras, and the roads should be just fine!'"

Annette folded the letter as she finished reading. "She's written a postscript almost as long as her letter, but it's all about somebody called Johnny Abbott, so I guess it's sort of a secret!"

Her aunt looked startled. "I hope Tonia isn't getting serious about anyone at *her* age! She's just a child, only a few months older than you are!"

Annette wrinkled her nose, but she didn't let Aunt Lila see that. "Yes, Auntie," she said, demurely. "I'm sure it's only for laughs!"

"Still, I wonder if I should write your aunt Betta and sort of mention the boy's name—"

"Aunt Lila!" Annette was genuinely horrified. "Tonia would think I showed you her letter! She'd never, ever forgive me! I'd die!"

Her aunt looked startled. "All right, dear." She waved her hands feebly in token of surrender. "I promise not to mention him." And she added, as an afterthought, "It is probably just temporary anyhow."

"That's almost for sure!" Annette grinned. For the last few years, pretty blond Tonia had written about a new crush in practically every other letter to Annette. The objects of her affections came and went far too fast for anyone to keep track of them, and each was, to quote Tonia herself, "positively the most utterly adorable" until he fell out of favor for one reason or another.

"Annette!" That was her uncle's voice. "You have company down here!"

"It's the gang!" exclaimed Annette, as a murmur of soprano voices belonging to her friends Babs, Nina, and

Teeny came wafting upward from the lower hall. "I'll be right back!" She flew down the hall to call from the top of the stairs, "Come on up and give me a hand!"

The three weren't much help with Annette's packing. They spent more time admiring her wardrobe than they did tucking it into the bags for her. But for the next half hour, the house was in a merry turmoil of chatter and laughter as each of the four told her own plans for the summer and promised solemnly to write all of the others about everything that happened during the long vacation.

Annette's aunt and uncle hated to break it up, but Annette had a long trip ahead of her, and it would be much easier for their niece at the other end of it if she could get to Lost Creek before dark. There were mountain roads to travel in the part of the state where the streams had once glittered with gold.

"Better get ready, dear. The service station man just brought your car." Her aunt had to speak loudly from the doorway to be heard over the racket of four young ladies all talking at once.

"I'm practically packed!" Annette called back. She and Teeny Travers were both sitting on top of the biggest suitcase so Babs and Nina could snap the locks shut on the bulging contents. "Now!" she commanded, but Babs and Nina were both giggling so much that they couldn't get the locks snapped together. They both let go and the lid popped open, sending Annette and Teeny sliding off onto the floor, arms and legs waving madly. Then all four collapsed in giggles.

"Uncle Archie will take care of that, dear. The girls had better run along now so you can get dressed." Aunt Lila looked at her watch. "I don't like to rush you away, girls, but Annette has a long way to go before dark."

"We're just leaving!" they chorused, but it took them another fifteen minutes before they were trooping out the front door, shouting good wishes back to Annette and reminding her to get back in time for the fall semester. Annette stood on the front steps of the pretty California home, waving to them as they piled into Teeny's station wagon.

Her own neat little white roadster, the Monster, Uncle Archie's birthday gift to her only a month earlier, stood glistening at the curb. The man from the gas station was talking to Uncle Archie and admiring the little sports car.

"Nice little job, this sports number." He patted the neat,

small hood. "Oughta take your niece anywhere she wants to go. She could drive to Alaska in this baby!"

"I hope she doesn't try!" Her uncle smiled wryly. "The Mother Lode country is far enough away for her to drive alone."

"Mother Lode, hey? Say, isn't that the part of the state where the old-timers found so much gold about a hundred years ago?"

"That's it. A lot of California history was made up in those Sierra foothills."

"I bet a guy could still get rich if he had time to go up there an' dig around!"

"Maybe!" Annette's uncle smiled. "But it's more likely that all he'd get would be some blisters and a lame back! That happened to a lot of men in the gold rush days, but history forgets them."

"Still, I'd sure like to try my luck—someday!" The gas station man looked dreamy. Then he grinned. "Some day when my kids are all grown up!"

He roared off a few minutes later on his delivery motorcycle, probably having forgotten all about it.

It was close to noon by the time Annette finally settled herself behind the wheel of the Monster and tooled the little white car out into the busy traffic of the Los Angeles streets.

It was a thrill to set out on such a long journey all alone. She had driven to all the interesting spots around the southern half of the state, sometimes with her aunt and uncle, other times with the car crowded with her girl-friends and followed by two or three other cars with the rest of the school gang. But this was different.

"At least I haven't a chance of getting lost!" She grinned, with a side glance at a sizable pile of maps on the seat beside her. Practically everyone, from Uncle Archie to the friendly postman, had presented her with a well-marked map. She had accepted them all gratefully, and no one's feelings had been hurt.

But I wish they'd stop treating me like an infant, she thought, just because I'm small! She'd had that problem for a long time. She *was* tiny, and it seemed to make everyone feel like protecting her.

That was what had driven her to learn to be expert in several athletic skills, to prove that even though she was small, she could keep up with the tall ones. She had become an expert swimmer, a good tennis player, and the best archer in her gang.

She sang happily to herself as she drove along the wide highway that led north. If she kept up a reasonable speed, stopping every two hours for a rest and a glass of milk or a candy bar, she would reach Lost Creek well before dark.

It would be fun to be with Tonia again. Her letters had been filled lately with news of meeting lots of interesting people in San Francisco, where the family spent each winter. She and Annette would have tons of things to talk about.

I hope she hasn't grown too much, Annette thought, frowning. Last time she mentioned how tall she was, she was two whole inches taller than I am! She had a sudden picture in her mind of a seven-foot-tall Tonia, with her own five-foot-two figure standing beside her cousin. The thought made her laugh, and she almost missed the large, new signs beside the road: DETOUR AHEAD. DRIVE SLOW. FIVE MILES OF CONSTRUCTION WORK. ONE LANE. NO PASSING.

And turning the next bend of the wide highway, she saw a long line of stopped cars in her lane, a flagman at its head. They were all waiting for an equally long line of cars to crawl past from the other direction, half hidden by a heavy cloud of dust.

She could only sit there and swallow the dust as it settled all over her and the pretty white sports car. And when the line started moving again, she had to crawl along behind a rickety truck loaded with household effects. The old truck was having enough trouble making the long rising grade of the paved highway. But when the bumpy detour began, it teetered and swayed and shook so violently that she expected to get part of its load in her lap at any moment.

*"Beep! Beep! Beep!"* It came from directly behind her—a gentle, inquiring *"beep!"*

Who was this joker? Trying to pass on a one-lane road! She turned to look back witheringly. But the driver of the very large and expensive car that towered over the rear of her poor little Monster wasn't trying to get past. He was smirking and waving flirtatiously, a big diamond on his pinky flashing in the sunlight.

She gave him a glare and turned back to her driving with a toss of the head.

There was no more beeping. "I guess that settled him!" She grinned to herself. And when the detour ended at last and she saw the THANK YOU FOR YOUR COURTESY sign, Annette shot ahead of the tottering truck and was soon out of the dust, with a clear, wide highway ahead.

It was good to be moving fast again. She looked at the dashboard clock. She would have to keep up a good speed to get to the foothills before the sun was so low in the west that it would almost blind her.

Then she heard the *beep! beep!* behind her again. It was quite close and she almost swerved to the edge of the road in her surprise. A quick glance in the rearview mirror showed her that it was the flirtatious gentleman with the diamonded pinky.

Annette put her foot on the accelerator so hard that the Monster half leaped off the ground. "Come on, Monster," she said with a chuckle, "let's get away from that big job!" And she sped away.

But the big car kept up easily, pacing the little car, now running ahead of it, now dropping back beside it. The driver was having a lot of fun showing off.

He dropped back to run alongside the Monster and smiled over at Annette. The freezing look that he got in return seemed to unnerve him so much that he sent the big car ahead at full throttle, and it roared away like a rocket. It must have been going ninety miles an hour as it disappeared around a turn in the highway.

"I'm glad we've seen the last of that character!" she confided to the Monster.

But they hadn't. A mile ahead, as Annette drove past at a strictly legal speed, she saw the big car drawn off the road and a grim-faced highway patrolman doggedly writing out a ticket for its driver, who was slumped unhappily in his seat with a face like a thundercloud.

Annette tried not to smile as she went by, but it was a lost effort. She *beep-beeped* faintly in salute as she drove out of sight.

In a little while she had come to the road that turned off the great valley highway and up, after a few more miles, into the Sierras. A few minutes to rest and walk about at a hamburger stand, and she was ready to start the long upward climb.

The road was still well surfaced for many miles and there was little traffic on it, so she made very good time. Gradually, she left the soft green fields of the valley behind and felt a cooler tinge in the summer air. There was a smell of sagebrush stirring.

A recent rain had drenched the low foothills and left a smell of dampness in the underbrush that skirted the narrowing road. Patches of wildflowers still made a colorful show under the spreading limbs of the sycamore trees. Cactus no longer showed itself in thick, unfriendly clumps. This was green, wooded country.

The sun was still high, but the tall mountains hid it and left the climbing road shadowed for long stretches. Soon, Annette noticed that the pale green sycamores had disappeared, and in their place, the dark green of juniper spread about in all directions, fragrant and sturdy, some still decked with pale blue berries from its winter fruiting. A sign said LOST CREEK — 30 MILES.

Now the road was narrow and she had to slow down. The Monster panted a little on the steep grade. And the shadows seemed darker on the road, which suddenly changed from paved to dirt.

The road was smooth enough, and well traveled, packed down under generations of wheels and tires, but there were treacherous patches of mud and water left by the rain.

Then, somehow, she found herself off the newer road and on a back road, one that probably only the locals used. Thinking back a few miles, she remembered one spot where an unmarked road had branched off at a sharp angle. But there had been no signpost, and she had kept straight on in the same direction she had been driving.

Now the Monster was really panting for breath, and Annette stopped at the top of a steep grade to give its motor a short rest. High above, the sky was still clear blue, but in the west it was shading to pink behind the tall peaks of the High Sierras, and some clouds to the east were catching and reflecting the pink and gold of sunset. She had better keep going while she could still see the road.

Slowly and carefully she drove up the narrow, twisting road till she came suddenly in sight of an ancient duster of wooden shacks nestled in a rock-lined, steep-sided canyon. A faded sign over the porch of the largest of the abandoned houses announced that it was the Applejack General Store. But its door and windows were boarded up, and in the other half dozen houses near the road, there was no sign of life. Now twilight had settled over all.

There was no use stopping, Annette thought. The empty houses, falling to pieces under their aged apple trees, were spooky! Whatever Applejack might once have been, it was only a ghost town now.

She drove on slowly, watching the narrow road as her headlights picked out the bumpy spots.

But in one of the old houses back from the road, an old, white-bearded man sat on a rickety porch and leaned forward, puffing at his pipe, to watch the small white sports car pass and disappear around a curve.

He waved his hand gravely after it and settled back in his rocking chair. "Jist keep on goin'!" he muttered, glaring in the direction the car had gone. "Seems like them durn ottymobiles can climb like cats these days. Feller can't git off by hisself nowhere!" And then, after a long time, he nodded glumly. "Reckon I'll hike myself up to the high country where it's peaceful!"

And then complete silence settled down again at the old mining town of Applejack.

In the light of the Monster's headlights, a small deer broke suddenly from the brush, leaped into the middle of the road, and stood staring, big-eyed, into the glare.

Annette managed to pull on the emergency brake in time to avoid hitting the hypnotized animal, but it still stood there, trembling.

She stood up and waved her arms over the top of the windshield. "Shoo, Bambi!" she called. "Shoo!"

And at the sound of her voice, the deer made two graceful leaps and disappeared into the dusk-shadowed brush.

"Thank goodness!" Annette sighed and then, laughing, called out after the departed one, "Bye, Bambi!"

Another turn in the road and around a shoulder of a hill, and there, unexpectedly, she saw a neat, modern road sign. LOST CREEK—2 MILES, it read. And looking past it, she saw a wide road leading down into a valley between two ranges of hills.

There was a faint twinkle of lights far in the valley. Lost Creek, at last! Soon she would be safe in Uncle Genio's pleasant home in the heart of the historic, gold rush town.

"We've made it, Monster, darling!" She patted the dusty dashboard and started down the road on the last stretch of her long journey. "We're there!"

But they weren't there yet.

# 2        *Cold Welcome*

It was long past seven o'clock and almost dark when Annette steered her little car down toward the lights of Lost Creek at the end of the valley.

She had been driving since noon, and she knew she'd be very glad when she could step out of the car in her uncle's driveway and relax.

Only two miles more to go!

Soon she began to pass isolated small houses set far back from the surfaced road. Faint yellow lamplight shone from some of the windows, and watchdogs barked distantly as her car went swiftly past.

Suddenly, there was a loud and ominous *whoosh* from the left rear tire, and the Monster settled down crookedly, bumping—*plop! plop!*—and veering crazily across the road.

She hung on to the steering wheel and fought desperately to keep the small car out of the roadside ditch. When she finally brought it to a stop, it was only inches from a two-foot drop into deep sand.

She climbed out to survey the damage. The tire and tube were a total loss.

Thank goodness I remembered to have the spare tire and tube tested when I filled up with gas! she thought. But when the car trunk was opened, Annette found she had no tools for tire changing. But they should be right here! she thought. She lifted out bags, moved her record player and her beach blanket, and dug around under an accumulation of summer things, including a pair of swim fins and a diving mask. But there was no jack to lift the Monster's wounded wheel. No tire wrench, either.

"Now what?" she asked the Monster glumly. "You must have devoured those tools! Aren't you ashamed of yourself?" She sat down on the edge of the open trunk, but got up again in a hurry as the Monster settled deeper into the sandy edge. "I take it all back! Please don't slide into the ditch!" She patted the white hood. "It's all my fault. I remember lending them to Babs when her brother drove over a pop bottle at the grunion hunt at Malibu Beach. Like a dope, I forgot to get them back!"

At least she knew where the tools were now. But it didn't help her change a tire on a lonesome road in a strange place.

She looked around and far up the road to the lights of Lost Creek. There were probably several gas stations there, but they wouldn't do her much good out here. The owners had probably closed up for the night, anyhow.

The small houses she had noticed a few minutes earlier were far behind now. All but one. She saw a light about a quarter of a mile away, among a cluster of buildings that looked like a house and barns. The place was set well back from the road and seemed quite small, among old, tall trees.

They might have a telephone, she thought hopefully. I can call Uncle Genio to come for me! And she set off quickly, without taking time to lock the trunk, though she did put her bags back before she started.

It wasn't far along the road to a spot where a driveway of a sort led back toward the tree-surrounded house and outbuildings. She could see, in the dim starlight, that the place was very old and run-down. A single kerosene lamp shone out into a white-fenced patch of garden in front of the house, and the window was half open.

Don't see a telephone pole around, she thought with a sinking heart. Maybe I should have gone back to one of the other houses. She paused, trying to decide whether to go on or turn back.

Then she heard someone start to sing. The sound was coming through the open window of the old house. The voice sounded familiar, and the song was a popular rock 'n' roll tune, backed by a sort of off-key harmonica instead of the usual guitar or "combo."

She thought she knew that voice. Timmy Taylor, the latest rave, had made a record of that song that had already sold more than a million copies.

Good! thought Annette. They've got a record player in there, so they probably have a phone, too! She hurried on, humming some harmony to the singing.

Her knock brought an abrupt end to the song. Heavy steps came to the door, and it was opened a few inches.

A tall young man frowned at her through the narrow opening. "Yes?" he asked curtly. "What is it?"

Annette smiled up at him. "I'm very sorry to bother you, but my car has a flat tire and I'd like to phone my family in Lost Creek."

"We don't have a phone. People up the road about half a mile have one—I think." He stepped back and made a motion as if to close the door in her face.

"Well, thanks for your help!" Annette's eyes flashed angrily. Chin in air, she started to turn away, but at that moment, a small girl came pushing past the unfriendly young man.

"Wait, please. Won't you come in?" She wasn't more than ten years old, a thin little thing with sandy hair in pigtails and a multitude of freckles across her turned-up nose. "If there's anything my brother and I can do for you, we'd be glad to. Wouldn't we, Stan?" She looked up appealingly at the tall young man's frowning face.

"Never mind," Annette answered shortly and started to turn away.

"Stan!" The small girl looked at him reproachfully. The young man shuffled his feet and looked embarrassed. "I'll go phone for you, if you want me to," he told Annette. "Won't take more'n ten minutes, if you'll wait here."

"Why, thank you very much!" Annette smiled up at him

gratefully. "I've been driving almost all day, and I don't know if I could walk half a mile!"

"Come on in!" The little girl pulled Annette inside the small living room and led her to the one comfortable chair. "Sit down, please."

Stan threw on a sweater. "Be right back," he told Annette.

"I'll play the harmonica for her!" his sister announced happily. And to Annette, "Do you like music?" She picked up an inexpensive harmonica from a table.

"Music! Ouch!" Stan grinned. "If you could just learn to stay on the right key!"

His sister made a face at him, but Annette was staring at him in surprise. "Was that you singing when I came up to the house?"

"Trying to," Stan admitted with a touch of shyness.

"I thought it was a Timmy Taylor record!" Annette told him. "You sing just like him."

"Stan sings lots better!" his little sister assured her solemnly. "Stan sings rock 'n' roll, an' country an' Western, an'—" She ran out of breath.

"Margie!" Stan was embarrassed. He changed the subject hastily. "I'll go make that call. What's the name of your folks in town?"

"Bori," Annette told him, smiling. "My uncle is Judge Bori. I'm going to spend the summer with them."

She was startled by the sudden change in both Margie's and her brother's faces. The friendliness faded out the moment she mentioned Judge Bori's name. They stared at her with enemy eyes.

Stan's voice was harsh. "I'm not running errands for Judge Bori or any part of his family!" He stalked toward the door. "Do your own phoning!" And a moment later he was gone into the darkness, slamming the door after him.

Annette was bewildered. "What hit him all of a sudden?" she asked.

Margie looked defiant. "We're the Turners. My father's Paul Turner!"

"Paul Turner?" Annette frowned, perplexed. "Should the name mean something to me?"

It was Margie's turn to look surprised. She studied Annette suspiciously for a moment. Then she shook her head slowly. "I guess you wouldn't know about it, living so far from Lost Creek. Judge Bori sent my father to prison a year ago."

"Oh! I'm sorry!" Annette couldn't think of anything better to say.

"Daddy didn't do what they said he did," Margie said firmly, "but he had to go to prison just the same—for a long, long time. And it was mostly Judge Bori's fault. He said terrible things about Daddy. He wouldn't believe him." Two big tears started to roll down the freckled cheeks.

Annette wished that she could say something to comfort the little girl. Maybe it would help to talk about something else. "Do you and your brother live here all alone?" she asked.

Margie sniffed back her tears and shook her head vigorously. "Mommy works at the Star Lunchroom, but she's home every night. She says it's no use blaming anybody, but Stan won't listen. He says people were against Daddy because he was poor—" A sob caught in her throat, and she rubbed her eyes with the back of her hand.

Annette sighed and stood up. "I'd better get started to the telephone. How far did your brother say that next house is?"

"'Bout half a mile," Margie told her, "toward town. It's a green-painted house. I'd go for you, but I'm not allowed to go out after dark."

"Oh, that's all right. Thanks just the same." Annette

patted her shoulder. "I won't mind the walk, now I've had a nice rest." And as she went toward the door, she called back, "Good-bye!"

"Bye," Margie called after her. "I'm sorry Stan wouldn't help."

"It's all right," Annette assured her kindly from the open doorway. "I guess I don't blame him, at that."

And as she went down the driveway toward the road to town, she was thinking, I suppose if *my* dad were sent to prison, I'd be sure he wasn't guilty, no matter what anybody said. And I guess I'd hate everybody who sent him there.

She looked back along the main road to where the Monster, a dark bulk, sat at the edge of the road. I wonder if I locked the trunk, she thought. Somebody might come along and decide to steal my new record player. Guess I'd better check.

She turned toward the car and walked briskly along the deserted road. It would take only a few minutes to make sure that her bags and the record player were locked up safely.

Her steps made no sound on the dirt road, and she was only a few yards away from the car when she heard a metallic clang from behind it. She stopped abruptly, listening. Another clang came—someone hammering on metal.

Annette's indignation rose. Somebody's stealing my hubcaps! she thought. They were special equipment, a birthday present from Aunt Lila, and very expensive.

She started running toward the car, without thinking of any danger from the thief. "Hey, there! Let my car alone!" she called.

It was Stan Turner who rose from beside the rear wheel, a tire iron in his hand. And when she got close enough for a good look, she saw that he had been changing her tire, using an old rusty jack.

"Oh! I—I thought you were someone stealing my hub-caps!" she explained apologetically. "I'm sorry. And thank you ever so much!"

But Stan quickly finished the tire change without answering, hurled the ruined tire into the open trunk, slammed down the lid of the trunk, and picked up his old jack before he turned to look at her.

"I wish you'd let me pay—" Annette started uneasily.

"Forget it. It's okay." He picked up the rest of his tools and started to turn away. Then he stopped, and she could see a smile, even in the half-dark of the stars. "Sorry I went off half-cocked back at the house. Guess I'm a little goofy—about some things."

"It's all right. I s'pose anybody'd feel that way," Annette replied.

He stared at her a moment, then mumbled, "Thanks. Good night."

He swung around abruptly and started off down the road in the direction of the Turner house.

"Good night, and *thank you!*" Annette called after him. "See you later!"

But Stan didn't look back or answer, and in a couple of minutes he had gone out of sight into the shadows of the roadside trees.

Annette was thoughtful as she climbed into the small car and backed it carefully away from the edge of the sandy road.

Once she had it pointed toward Lost Creek, she took off as rapidly as she dared on the dark road. And as she pressed her foot down hard on the pedal, she nodded to herself and said, "First chance I get, I'll ask Uncle Genio to tell me all about Mr. Turner. I hope it wasn't anything real grim that he did!"

# 3

## *Lost Creek*

There was an old covered bridge at the foot of the main street of Lost Creek, and even though Annette was late, she stopped the Monster and sat a few minutes, looking at the tumbling waters pouring down from the high peaks of the Sierras.

The stones in the creek bed rattled loudly as the fast current stirred them, and the sound was happily familiar. The water would be icy cold so early in summer, she remembered. Right under this end of the bridge, she and Tonia had found their very own hiding place. Here they had dabbled pink toes in the shallows and told their dreams and plans to each other, that long-ago summer.

The old bridge creaked and groaned as she drove onto

the ancient flooring, but she didn't worry. It had stood there a hundred years, and would stand a hundred more, if they didn't pull it down, plank by plank, timber by timber.

In a region rich with legends of gold rush days, the town of Lost Creek had made more than its share of history. It was a sleepy little place for several months of the year, but in spring and summer it came alive. And its Pioneer Days celebration brought hundreds of tourists to join in the fun of turning back the clock.

This year, Lost Creek was planning to outdo itself, because this was the centennial of the first gold strike in its history.

As she drove down narrow Main Street, Annette saw that most of the decorations were already in place for the weekend start of the celebration. Red, white, and blue bunting hung from one side of the street to the other, decorated with banners proclaiming the dates of the Pioneer Days.

There were lights in several of the stores, and she noticed that people were decorating their windows with posters. The door of old Firehouse Number Two was open, and the old-timers were sitting around inside as usual, smoking their pipes. The ancient structure was part museum now and housed only the obsolete steam fire engine that no longer guarded the safety of Lost Creek. Annette knew that, around the corner on a newer street, there was a modern firehouse, with the latest type of equipment and an alert fire department ready for all emergencies. Her uncle, Judge Bori, had donated both the firehouse and the equipment to his hometown.

She felt a pang as she passed the old First Church with its ivy-covered brick walls and the supporting timbers that had been brought around the Horn in a sailing ship. Someone had put up a shiny modern gasoline station next door to the church, and a radio was raucously blaring one of the noisier rock 'n' roll records.

But, as she turned up the side street toward her uncle's home on the hill overlooking the center of town, she left the noise behind her. The Bori place, two stories high, sat in the midst of an old apple orchard planted by the original Bori family, four generations ago. A circular driveway lined with rhododendron bushes led up to the house.

Her uncle and his family had a home in San Francisco, but he had never given up his residence in Lost Creek. He was very proud of his town, and for part of each winter and during all of the summer months, he presided over its superior court.

Annette hoped no one had been worried because she had taken so long to arrive. She *beep-beeped* her horn as she pulled up in front of the tall porch steps.

The front door opened with a bang, and Tonia came running out and down the steps, blond ponytail bouncing.

"Annette! I told Mom and Dad you'd get here okay! They were just getting ready to call your Uncle Archie long distance to see if you'd eloped!" She giggled excitedly and threw her arms around Annette before her cousin was all the way out of the seat. "I'm so glad you're here!"

"Me, too!" Annette replied, returning the hug.

Now they stood face-to-face, looking each other over searchingly. "You look just the same!" they said together, as if they had rehearsed it. Then they laughed again and had to hug each other once more.

"Of course, you've grown lots," Tonia said frankly, "but I'm still a few inches taller."

"Not as much as you used to be!" Annette said with a happy grin. "Am I glad! Now they can't call us Beanpole and Shorty!"

"Goodness, I'd forgotten that!" Tonia laughed. "Don't breathe those horrible names!"

"Don't worry! I won't!" Annette assured her with a grimace. "I'm five foot two now, and anybody who calls me Shorty will be slain right off!"

Mike, the ancient handyman, came hurrying around a corner of the house. "Miss Annette! It's fine to see you again!" But he looked doubtfully at the Monster. "What's this critter you're drivin'? Is it safe for an old horseman to tackle?"

"He's tame as a lamb!" Annette assured him, patting the Monster's hood. "Monster, this is Mike. You be nice to him now!"

"Hm-m-m!" Mike wasn't entirely convinced. He took her car keys and started to unload her bags. The latest model in which Mike had any faith was a '29 Ford.

The girls went up the steps with their arms around each other, chattering a blue streak.

Tonia's father and mother were in the high-ceilinged front parlor, waiting to greet Annette. Eugenio Bori was nearing middle age, his black hair streaked with gray. The dignified judge was always a little bewildered by his pretty blond daughter and her teenage pals, who seemed to troop in and out of the historic Bori mansion without regard for peace and dignity.

Trim, lively Aunt Betta was always ready to help Tonia and her friends have a good time. She was delighted to have Annette there for the summer. She felt that Annette's common sense would balance Tonia's flightiness.

Aunt Betta had a hug and kiss for Annette, and Uncle Genio welcomed her with his usual reserve. But Annette knew he was glad to see her, and she promptly threw her arms around his neck and kissed him heartily on both cheeks, which brought a happy chuckle from Uncle Genio, who had been hoping she'd do just that.

The clock in the library was chiming, and there was a sound of pots and pans being rattled in the kitchen. "Goodness!" Aunt Betta exclaimed. "Honey, take Annette right up to her room so she can wash up for dinner. Katey's been fussing for an hour because the roast is getting dried out!" There was another crash of pans from the kitchen.

"Okay, Mom!" Tonia grabbed Annette's hand and the two of them raced up the staircase, just as they had done years ago when their heads had been barely higher than the stair rail.

"Do I get my same room?" Annette was breathless as they reached the top of the stairs.

"Silly! Of course you do!" Tonia replied. "Your 'Chamber of Horrors'!"

They both laughed, remembering when Katey, then the upstairs maid, had come into Annette's room to clean on that morning so many years ago, and had come rushing out again, yelling for help. Annette's collection of tadpoles had suddenly graduated overnight into frogs and were hopping about all over the room. City-raised Katey had refused to go back in there till the girls had gathered up every last one of them, and even then she had taken her broom along for protection.

The pleasant bedroom, with its old-fashioned lace curtains, was just as Annette remembered it. Even the horsehair sofa, which had prickled the unwary youngster who sat down on it in a scanty bathing suit, was still in its corner. And the wide bed, with its half-canopy of white linen and heavy lace edging, still dominated the room.

Annette stood in the doorway and threw out her arms as if to catch the whole room in a hug. "I love it!" she told Tonia breathlessly. "I'm so glad I could come!"

"And I'm glad, too!" Tonia's blue eyes sparkled. "We'll have a ball this summer! There are some simply fabulous characters here!"

Annette smiled teasingly. "Would one of them be named Johnny Abbott?"

"Oh!" Tonia's checks got red. "Did I mention him in my letter?"

"Just one page full, that's all!" Annette teased.

Tonia pouted reproachfully. "You can laugh, but wait till you meet him! He's tall—and good-looking—and his hair's naturally wavy!" She sighed dreamily. "And he sings!"

"He sounds thrilling!" Annette's dark eyes twinkled mischievously. He was probably a goon, she decided, but she'd have to make believe she was impressed. She knew Tonia's crushes were always "the most"—while they lasted.

"Girls!" Aunt Betta called up the stairs. "Stop chattering! Mike is on his way up with your bags, Annette. And dinner's almost on the table. Tonia, come down here! You two can visit later!"

"Tell you all about him after dinner!" Tonia promised hastily, and ran out, almost bumping into old Mike as he laboriously carted Annette's record player and three heavy bags into the room.

"Here y'are," he announced, plopping them down on the bed. "Looks like you'll be having music."

"All the latest!" Annette replied.

Mike shook his head disapprovingly. "Beats me what you young'uns call music. Just plain caterwaulin', some of it!" And he shuffled out of the room.

Annette laughed and then sobered. Speaking of singing, she mustn't forget to ask her uncle about Stan Turner's father, and why the young singer was so bitter.

Her chance seemed to be at hand when Katey set down the dessert and left the quiet dining room with a trayful of dishes. Tonia had rattled on all during the meal about old friends and new in Lost Creek and the lovely plans she had made for Annette and herself.

For a moment, Tonia was absorbed in raspberry sherbet and one of Katey's homemade cookies.

"Uncle Genio," Annette began, "remember I told you that an awfully obliging boy changed my flat tire?"

Her uncle looked at her inquiringly. "Why, yes. Don't tell me you forgot to pay the fellow!"

"He wouldn't take it," Annette explained, "but that isn't

what I mean. I mean—his name was *Stanley Turner*." She studied her uncle's face to see his reaction to the name, but Judge Bori only looked puzzled.

"So?" he asked with an inquiring smile.

Annette didn't quite know how to go on. Her aunt and Tonia were staring at her, waiting for her to explain. "I—I thought you'd know him, maybe," she said a little weakly.

"Goodness! The town's full of strangers!" Tonia offered. "He's probably here for the celebration!"

"No." Annette shook her head soberly. "He lives here."

"Turner?" Uncle Genio knitted his brows, then suddenly sat back in his chair. Annette could see that he was remembering the name now.

But the doorbell was ringing loudly, and Tonia was on her feet in a flash. "It's the kids!" she announced excitedly. "I asked a bunch of them to come over and meet Annette." And she ran out to the hall.

"Oh, no!" her mother groaned. "The poor child is too tired to bother with them tonight. Aren't you, dear?"

"Not at all, Aunt Betta," Annette said quickly. She was disappointed at the interruption, just when Uncle Genio had remembered, but she had to be polite.

Aunt Betta rose determinedly. "I'm going to shoo them down to the playroom. You sit right there and finish your dessert before you go down." And then she, too, was gone.

Uncle Genio waited till the door to the hall had closed behind Aunt Betta. Then he leaned forward and asked Annette gravely, "Paul Turner's son?"

"Yes, Uncle Genio." She nodded, her face sober. "His little sister told me that you—that is, his father is in prison—and you—they were all upset when they found out I was related to you—" She was floundering, with her uncle's eyes fixed steadily on her face.

A grim little smile twisted the corner of Judge Bori's mouth, but his eyes were stern. "I think I can guess what they had to say. I heard it all when I sentenced their father to twenty years in State Prison."

"Twenty years!" Annette was horrified. "But what did he do?"

"Didn't they tell you?" he asked, studying her.

Annette shook her head. "Only that—whatever it was—he didn't do it."

"The jury thought otherwise. And I must admit that in light of the evidence presented, I agree with the jury."

"Oh," Annette answered weakly. "But what *was* it?"

"Robbery! And possibly murder!" Judge Bori was stern. "Turner robbed an old prospector of his life savings, a miserable bag of nuggets worth less than a hundred dollars. And he had the brazen effrontery to try to cash in those nuggets at the store where the old man had been dealing for forty years!"

Annette swallowed hard. "Y-you said—*murder*. Did he kill the prospector? Are you sure?"

"I'm afraid there's little doubt of it. The body hasn't been found yet, but all the evidence pointed to Turner's having committed the crime in the old man's cabin, up in the High Sierras. There are a dozen deep canyons near it where a body could lie hidden for years."

He saw the shocked look on Annette's face and was sorry that he had said as much as he had. "Forget it, child. It's natural for any man's family to feel the way the Turners evidently do. But this is one case where I firmly believe that justice was done!"

"Annette! Aren't you through eating *yet*?" Tonia poked her head in at the door to the hall. "The kids are waiting to meet you!"

"Be right there!" Annette folded her napkin hurriedly and pushed back her chair. She hesitated a moment, before starting away from the table, and met her uncle's eyes soberly. "Thank you for telling me, Uncle Genio. But I still hope the Turners are right and there's been a mistake."

Judge Bori sighed. "That's your privilege, child. But I'm afraid it's a wasted hope."

# 4        *Tonia's Crush*

As Tonia brought her cousin into the basement playroom, the four boys and two girls gathered around a tall upright piano stopped singing and turned toward Annette.

"Here she is!" Tonia announced from the doorway, and a minute later was rattling off introductions so rapidly that Annette hardly caught the names. For the moment, there were just six new faces, all smiling, and all saying, "Hi, Annette!" "How are you?" "Glad to know you!" in assorted sopranos and baritones.

"Please, don't stop," she urged, gesturing toward the piano. "It sounded great!"

"Come on and join in!" A tall young man with wavy blond hair, who had been playing rather haltingly, rose from the piano bench and was striding over to her.

Before she realized what he intended to do, he had taken her by the hand and was drawing her rapidly toward the piano. "Tonia says you're a piano whiz! Have my seat, madam!" he said with a laugh.

"I'd rather listen for a while." Annette stopped abruptly and released her hand. She didn't want them to think that she wished to be coaxed, but she didn't intend to be pressured into showing off. "Please!"

"Don't rush the gal, Johnny!" the boy who had been introduced as Tim Carroll drawled. "We can stand your playing for a while yet!"

"You can go jump in the creek!" Johnny retorted and sprawled in a chair, scowling. "I've had enough beefs."

"Oh, Johnny, Tim didn't mean it!" Tonia seemed worried, Annette thought. "Please play some more for us."

So, that's the fabulous Johnny! Annette thought. Sulking worse than a seven-year-old because he hadn't gotten his way. He *was* good-looking, but unless she was very much mistaken, he knew it!

Now Tonia and the girl she had introduced as Lola Wagner had Johnny by the arms and were dragging him to his feet and over toward the piano. He was getting over his sulks and laughing as they alternately pulled and pushed him across the room.

Annette sat down some distance from the piano and was surprised to see the other three boys exchanging disgusted looks, aiming them toward Johnny. She heard Deke Jensen, the solemn-faced, spectacled one, say, "Some people like Roquefort."

"And some like Gorgonzola," Tim Carroll answered with a straight face.

"You never can tell," they said together, and solemnly nodded.

"So be it!" Kerry Harris said, and all three nodded.

Annette stifled a grin. She didn't need a diagram to know how they felt about Johnny's act.

The girls had him seated at the piano now, and he was running the scales lightly, while they tried to decide which song they wanted to try next.

"Okay, everyone. Come on, Annette, you know this one!" Tonia called out. And Johnny started the introduction to "The Roving Gambler," one of the songs that they intended to sing at the square dance that was to be the biggest event of the Pioneer Days.

Annette wasn't sure of the words, so she waited till they

had sung it a couple of times before she joined in the chorus of the old song.

When they had finished, Johnny swung around on the bench and grinned at her. "That was keen!"

"Smooth!" Deke agreed, beaming at Annette. "Your voice is just what we needed! Why don't we work up a specialty? Maybe a Spanish number!"

Johnny was ad-libbing eagerly, ignoring Tonia's sudden pout. "I'll do the *caballero* with my guitar, and you sing," he told Annette. "Hey, let's do 'Juanita'! The rest of you kids can hum the background for us!"

There was a clamor of approval from everyone except Tonia, but when Johnny turned to her questioningly, she managed a smile. "Sounds wonderful!"

So they began to rehearse it, with Annette singing the verse and Johnny strumming his guitar and joining in on the chorus, while the others harmonized.

And by the time Mrs. Bori called down to them that the hot chocolate and cookies were ready in the kitchen, for a good-night snack, they had the whole song worked out.

A little later, as the guests left noisily, crowded into Johnny's expensive convertible, Annette and Tonia stood together, waving after them from the front porch.

"They're a lot of fun, all of them," Annette told her cousin, as the big car sped out of sight and they started back into the house.

"Did you like Johnny?" Tonia asked. "Isn't he terrific?"

Annette hesitated. She wanted to be perfectly honest. "I guess so," she said with a smile. "He certainly comes on strong!"

Tonia frowned. "I mean, don't you think he's the best-looking thing you ever saw?" She studied Annette almost anxiously.

Annette yawned. She was tired after the long day, and right then it didn't matter to her what Johnny Abbott looked like. "I dunno," she said sleepily. "I suppose he's better-looking than the other three."

Tonia took a deep breath and then smiled. Annette's words seemed to reassure her. "I like him—a lot."

They were putting out the hall lights and locking the house. Annette looked over at Tonia as her cousin was speaking. She could see that Tonia meant it. I'd better not criticize him. I might hurt her feelings, she thought. And, aloud, she said, "I don't remember a boy by that name when we were small. Is he a local?"

"Goodness, no! His dad's a big stockbroker in the

capital, and his mother's traveling in Europe. They're horribly rich!" Tonia explained, as they went up the stairs. "He's going to Switzerland this fall—if he doesn't sign a contract with a record company!"

"A contract! To *sing*?" Annette hadn't thought his voice was that good or unusual.

"Why, of course! Don't you just *love* his voice?" she asked breathlessly. "He's going to win the singing contest! Everybody thinks so."

"At the celebration?" Annette asked.

Tonia nodded, her eyes sparkling. "He says there'll be scouts from the record companies listening. The contest may even be on radio! Won't that be exciting?"

"Uh-huh!" Annette was too sleepy to be excited about anything but her nice soft bed. She halted in front of her door. "Good night, Tone! What's getting-up time?"

"Whenever you feel like it!" Tonia replied. "But don't forget we have a date at ten to go riding with the gang!"

"I'll try to pull myself together by then, but the way I feel now, I'll be lucky to wake up by noon!"

But both of them were up hours before the rest of the riding party were due. Aunt Betta saw to that. And she kept after them till they were dressed in their riding clothes: white shirts, khaki breeches, and jodhpur boots.

Katey fixed packages of sandwiches for them and tucked in a treat or two before she closed their lunch boxes.

"Don't go too far or stay too late. Remember, tomorrow is another day," Aunt Betta warned them as they ran off to the barn to get their horses.

Old Mike had remembered that Annette had learned to ride on Chieftain. He'd been up since dawn, grooming the handsome gray horse, as well as the spirited little buckskin that was Tonia's favorite.

As Annette and Tonia came into the dim coolness of the barn, Annette gave a squeal of delight at the sight of Chieftain saddled in his stall, his sleek gray coat shining.

She ran and threw her arms around Chieftain's neck. The big horse whinnied and nuzzled her shoulder with his soft nose. "He remembers me!" she called out happily. "Look! He's begging for sugar—and I forgot to bring it!"

Mike came up, grinning. "Here!" He gave her a handful of lump sugar for the big gray.

"Thanks, Mike! I hope he'll forgive me for being so forgetful!" Chieftain reached over and took the whole handful at once and crunched it contentedly.

"Come see Eagle, or he'll be jealous!" Tonia called, stroking her favorite and laying a cheek against his neck.

A shadow fell across the open doorway and they saw Johnny riding in. Outside in the sunlight, Deke and Tim were riding up, with Lola Wagner in her smart tailor-made outfit.

Johnny sat his mount with style, and Annette had to admit that he made a handsome picture as he reined in and looked at them challengingly.

"Hi, chicks!" He waved a silver-mounted riding whip. When he saw that he had the attention of both of them, he pulled on the reins and made his horse stand up on its hind legs, pawing the air.

Annette knew he was showing off, but when she stole a quick glance at Tonia, she saw Tonia looking at him in wide-eyed awe and admiration as he brought the horse down and made it wheel and kick up its hind legs.

Tonia gave an excited little cry and pretended to be frightened as she backed away, but Annette stood her ground, watching calmly.

"Whoa, Dusty!" Johnny brought the horse to a standstill and made a graceful dismount. "Don't be afraid.

I had him under control!" he told Annette and Tonia with a little swagger.

"Gracious!" Tonia shuddered. "I was scared!"

But Annette looked over at old Mike and caught his eye. He winked broadly and let a grin twist the corner of his mouth before he went to lead the girls' horses out of their stalls. Annette had to hide a smile as she prepared to mount Chieftain. She could have made her horse do exactly the same routine as Johnny's, if she had wanted to. And she knew that Tonia could have done it with Eagle! And old Mike knew it, too—having taught it to both of them that long-ago summer!

Annette made a hasty mount as she saw Johnny striding over to help her. Then she wheeled Chieftain and trotted him out into the sunshine to join the other riders.

She caught a glimpse of Johnny's face as she rode past him. He was wearing that "spoiled brat" frown again.

But a couple of minutes later, when he and Tonia rode out of the barn, side by side, they were both smiling, and Tonia was tossing her blond ponytail and fluttering her lashes flirtatiously at him.

"Blast off for Morgan Hill!" Johnny called out, and he and Tonia galloped their horses down the back road that wound around through the foothills and then up into the more rugged hills where the big gold mines had been.

The others followed, Deke and Tim riding side by side, cameras swinging from their shoulders. Annette and Lola brought up the rear at a more leisurely pace.

"What's Morgan Hill?" Lola called to Annette as they trotted their mounts along a level stretch.

"I've read that it was one of the richest 'diggings' in the whole district," Annette told her. "At one of the mines, they took out a nugget that weighed a hundred and ninety-five pounds, solid gold, worth over forty-three thousand dollars!"

"Whew!" Lola whistled boyishly.

"Uncle Genio says there were hundreds of cabins around here, crowded together, a month after that. You'd never guess it now, would you?"

There were few signs of that gold rush now—only an occasional skeleton of a shack, high above the trail.

"Why did they call these hills the 'Mother Lode'?" Lola asked. "I know a lode is a mineral deposit in the rocks. But why *mother*?"

"Well, for a couple of years people believed that there was a mile-wide ribbon of pure gold, a hundred and twenty miles long, running through these foothills. They thought that the nuggets on the banks of the creeks and in the riverbeds had broken off from that main or 'mother' lode, and all they'd have to do was dig a few feet to find it!"

"No wonder they flocked here!" Lola exclaimed. "Did they find out there was no such golden ribbon?"

"There wasn't *one* fabulous one, but there were enough smaller veins to make a lot of people rich, till all of a sudden they couldn't find any more. Then they had to tunnel deeper and deeper, and the ore kept getting poorer and harder to bring out. Soon it was only the big operators with expensive machinery and big stamp mills for extracting the gold from the ore that could make a profit."

"Is the gold all gone now?" Lola asked.

"I guess it never will be. Uncle Genio says people still come and dig, though hardly any of them ever find enough gold to buy groceries. But they keep on digging."

"It would be fun to try to find a nugget in the creek!" Lola suggested eagerly. "Why don't we someday?"

"That's a keen idea!" Annette agreed eagerly. She would love to have a souvenir nugget to show her friends down home. "I'll see what Tonia thinks about it!"

They had gradually dropped back quite a distance from the rest of the party, and now as they started up a steep bit of trail, Annette felt Chieftain go suddenly lame. She pulled up at once and swung out of her saddle.

"It's probably a pebble caught in his shoe," she guessed. "I'd better take care of it right now."

Lola pulled up, waiting, as Annette examined the big gray's front right hoof. It took only a minute to dig out the offending piece of rock, but when Chieftain set his foot down, he still seemed to be uncomfortable.

"I'd better let him rest a few minutes," Annette decided. "You go on ahead and tell the others I'll be along soon. I see a nice little spring over there in those rocks and Chieftain might like a drink."

Far up the trail, they heard Deke yelling back at them to come on and quit holding up the parade.

"We're coming!" Lola called to him, but she still hesitated to leave Annette alone.

"Go ahead. And tell Deke to stop bellowing. He's disturbing the peace!" Annette smiled and pointed to a miniature slide at the side of the trail, where a small furry gray animal was frantically trying to climb the piled-up rocks, but kept slipping and sliding back in his fright.

"Oh, the cutie! What is it?" Lola rode over to get a closer look at the little round-eared ball of fur. And as she did, he slid back and fell to the ground, letting out an agonized *"eeenk-eeenk!"* like a shrill whistle. At once, there were several other *eeenk-eeenk* whistles from different directions, and the small fugitive whisked out of sight into the brush.

Annette laughed. "That was a pika, a 'rock rabbit' some people call him. He's awfully shy."

"He certainly had his friends around to give him advice! I never heard such whistling!" Lola said with a laugh.

"The funny part of it is that there probably wasn't another pika anywhere around here. He made all that noise himself. Pikas are natural-born ventriloquists. That's how they keep from being caught, I've heard. Their enemies don't know which way to look for them!"

"It *must* be confusing to a hungry weasel!" Lola agreed.

This time it was Johnny Abbott's voice calling impatiently that disturbed the tranquil silence of the trail.

"I'd better hurry, before the Greek god gets angry!" Lola said with a mischievous smile.

"That would never do!" Annette agreed with a grin.

And a moment later, when Lola rode on, Annette was still chuckling at the description of Tonia's "crush." That's probably what he thinks he looks like, at that! she thought.

She led Chieftain, still limping, over to the tall boulders where a small spring was bubbling out of a fissure to fall splashingly into a tiny roadside pool. "Come on, you big faker," she scolded the gray horse playfully. "You're just stalling so you can steal a rest! I'll give you three minutes, no more!"

He drank noisily, and Annette told him, "I don't think much of your table manners, but I think I'll join you. I'm too thirsty to be fussy!"

She waited till Chieftain had finished and had moved a couple of feet away to crop some fresh green grass at the side of the trail. Then she leaned over and held her face up under the dripping spring, so that the water splashed down into her mouth. It also splashed all over her face and into her hair, but she didn't mind. It was so refreshingly cool that she caught handfuls and threw them on her face, enjoying the icy sting although it took her breath away.

Chieftain whinnied suddenly, and Annette turned hastily to see what had caused it.

She was amazed to see, only a few feet away in the

brush, a tall young man watching her. He was wearing an old leather jacket, short in the sleeves and evidently long outgrown, and his blue denim trousers were faded and patched. He was carrying a knapsack over one shoulder and an old fishing pole over the other.

It was Stanley Turner.

# 5 *Stan Turner's Story*

Annette was so surprised to see Stan Turner way up there on the hill trail that for a moment she just stood and stared at him without a word. But when she saw a slow grin dawning on his face, her own cheeks turned pink. She realized what a sight she must be, dripping wet, with her hair plastered down over her forehead.

"Oh, hello," she said faintly. "I was getting a drink."

Stan's grin grew wider. "Looked more like you were taking a shower!"

"Feels like it, too!" Annette said with a laugh as a cascade of drops ran down her nose and dripped off.

"Here!" Stan swung the knapsack around and pulled out a clean towel. "Mop off with this."

"Thanks!" Annette took it and tried to dry some of the water off her face. "Br-r-r! It's icy!"

"Better sit over there on the rock in the sun and dry out a while. Your friends will think you fell into a puddle headfirst!"

"Oh! Did you see them go by?" She sat down on the rock and shook her damp curls in the warm sunshine.

"Who could miss them, the way Deke was bellowing!" Stan replied.

"Why, do *you* know Deke?" She was surprised and pleased.

Stan sobered instantly, and the scowl she had seen the night before replaced his friendly smile. "Why shouldn't I know him?" he demanded belligerently.

Annette was startled. "No reason," she said. "I just didn't think—I mean, Deke's a summer visitor, and—"

Stan interrupted rudely. "You mean because my father's in prison, you think I'm not good enough to know your friends!" He glared at her.

She was angry, and at the same time, she couldn't help feeling sorry for Stan. She looked steadily at him for a moment before she spoke. "It's too bad you think so, Stan

Turner. I don't feel that way at all." Then her eyes flashed angrily. "But if *you* go around feeling sorry for yourself all the time, nobody'll want to know *you*!"

She flung the damp towel to him, got up, and went to her horse. "Come on, Chieftain," she said. "Let's go!" And she started to mount.

"Wait, please!" Stan hurried over. "I'm sorry. I didn't really mean it. It's just that things get me down sometimes."

Annette paused, with her hand on Chieftain's bridle, and studied the tall young man a moment. "I know," she replied. "Uncle Genio told me what the charges were against your father."

"Did he tell you my father's side?" Stan demanded bitterly.

"He didn't have time," Annette answered gravely. "We were interrupted."

"He didn't believe my father anyhow. But *I* know the truth!" His hands were clenched at his sides, his eyes begging Annette to believe him.

"Would you tell me about it? I honestly would like to hear."

Stan hesitated. Annette could see that he wanted

to tell her but was afraid she wouldn't believe him.

"Please?" She smiled. "Let's both sit down on that rock while I dry my hair."

"Okay!" Stan had made up his mind.

They sat down, and Annette bent her head and ran her fingers through her thick curly hair, shaking out the spring water. "Go ahead," she told him.

"Well," he plunged into the story, "Dad was always dreaming about finding that Mother Lode up here. That's why we moved to Lost Creek six years ago from Missouri. People in town thought he was just lazy and shiftless, but it wasn't so. He just was so sure that he could find it that nothing else seemed to matter. I guess you'd say that he had gold fever."

"Lots of people have had that," Annette conceded, "and they found gold. Did he?"

"A little, now and then. But never anything worth the hard labor he put into digging for it." Stan shook his head and sighed. "Then two years ago, he met this old character somewhere out in these hills. I guess they'd call him a hermit type. His name was Joe Robbins, and he must have been prospecting here and there in these mountains for fifty or sixty years, and doing pretty well."

"Did he help your father find any gold?" Annette asked eagerly.

"Just the opposite! He told Dad to stay out of the hills or he'd run into trouble. And a couple of weeks later, when Dad saw him in the grocery store at Lost Creek buying supplies, they had a quarrel because Dad said he'd prospect anywhere he wanted to, so long as it was government-owned land."

"Did he go back where the old man was?"

Stan nodded grimly. "A few days later, he was digging in the hills above Loon Lake when somebody took a shot at him with a rifle. Just missed him, too. Dad ducked behind a tree and looked around to see who was shooting at him."

"Was it the old prospector?" Annette asked breathlessly.

"Nobody else! Dad spotted him climbing a big rock a couple hundred feet away so he could see where his target was hiding. But when old Robbins got to the top, he jumped to his feet, yelling, and started clubbing something with his rifle butt."

"Goodness! Was he crazy?"

"Crazy scared! He'd been bitten by a big rattlesnake that had been lying on top of the rock, sunning itself."

"Ugh!" Annette shuddered and glanced around hastily to be certain there weren't any of them within striking distance. "What did your dad do?"

"The old man was holding his jaw and yelling for help, and Dad guessed right away what had happened. So he ran to help him."

"Did he save his life?"

Stan nodded soberly. "He had a snake-bite kit with him, and he pulled old Robbins through somehow. He stuck with him for two days and nights till he was out of danger. It was a tough battle."

"But if he saved Mr. Robbins's life, why did the jury say just the opposite?" Annette was indignant.

"It was the little leather bag of nuggets that made them do that. Robbins insisted on giving it to Dad for what he had done. At first, Dad wouldn't take it, but he was almost broke and finally he let the old guy talk him into it. Robbins boasted he knew where to get plenty more when he needed it."

"And then," Annette said soberly, "when he tried to buy things with the gold, your father was accused of robbery and—killing the old man. That's what Uncle Genio told me."

"He should know!" There was bitterness in Stan's

voice. "Dad explained what had happened, but hardly anyone except us believed him. And when the old-timer didn't come in for supplies for a long while, your uncle sent Police Chief Trujillo up to the shack at Loon Lake to see if he was still there and would back up my father's story about how he got the nuggets."

"But he wasn't there. . . ." Annette supplied softly.

"That's right," Stan agreed miserably, "and no one has seen him since. And to make it worse, the cabin door was open and everything inside was smashed as if there had been a terrible fight! So they blamed it on Dad. And the jury agreed."

"I can see how it would look to them," Annette said honestly. "What do you think happened up there after your dad left?"

"Old Robbins could have wandered off to one of his other diggings and forgotten to board up the shack. A hungry bear might have gotten in and wrecked the place. That's happened before."

"Did you tell them that?" she asked eagerly.

Stan nodded. "I tried. But nobody would buy it."

"I don't see why not!" Annette declared. She was indignant. "It makes a lot of sense!"

Stan Turner smiled at her gratefully. "Seems so to me," he agreed. "That's why I come up here whenever I can, hoping to run into the old guy somewhere. I know I can get him to come down to Lost Creek with me if I can locate him."

"I certainly hope you find him!" Annette smiled back at Stan as she arose from the rock where they had been sitting. Her hair was dry now, in soft ringlets. She realized that she had better be hurrying on to join her friends at Morgan Hill before they decided she had fallen off the trail and came back to find her. "I guess I'd better start riding. My hair is nice and dry now."

"Gosh! I didn't mean to bend your ear this long!" Stan was embarrassed as he stood twisting his dusty old hat in his hands.

"Please, I'm the one who asked the questions." Annette smiled. "And I'm awfully glad we ran into each other again. Honestly!" She put out her hand impulsively, and Stan took it in a firm clasp.

"It's too bad I didn't bring my camera!" a voice said from a few yards up the trail.

They turned, startled, to see Johnny Abbott on Dusty, watching with a sarcastic smile. They broke apart, both a

little self-conscious, and watched as Johnny came riding down the trail toward them.

When he was still a dozen feet away, he struck the horse with his silver-mounted riding whip, and the big animal leaped forward so violently that Stan, in its direct path, had to jump backward to avoid being run down.

As he did so, he stumbled on a soft spot in the sand at the side of the trail, and it threw him off balance. For a moment, he struggled to keep on his feet, but the sand gave way under them, and he toppled back against the brush and crashed full length.

Johnny wheeled his horse and came back. The sight of Stan struggling to get to his feet struck him as so funny that he sat laughing.

"That was a showboat trick!" Annette's eyes flashed as she glared up at him.

Johnny stopped laughing at once and swung out of his saddle. He strode over to where Stan was awkwardly getting up and put out a hand to help him.

But Stan was in a rage. He was certain that Johnny had deliberately made him look foolish, and he ignored the outstretched hand and aimed a wild blow at its owner.

Johnny sidestepped, and the angry Stan spun half around before he could regain his balance and gather himself for another try.

"Sorry, old fellow!" Johnny drawled. "I really didn't mean to run you down." His words were friendly enough, but they didn't sound as if he meant them.

Stan caught the undertone, and his face reddened with anger. But before he could aim a second blow at Johnny's faintly smiling face, Annette spoke up quickly. "Please, Stan—" she said, and he let his fist drop to his side.

"Johnny Abbott," she said, stepping between them, "this is Stan Turner."

The two boys stared into each other's faces, Johnny still wearing a faint, supercilious smile and Stan scowling uncertainly.

"I know," Johnny said carelessly. "I've seen him around. Hi!" The last was grudging.

Stan nodded without speaking, his eyes still hostile.

Annette felt the tension in the air. "I think we'd better get started," she told Johnny hurriedly. "I'm sorry I kept the kids waiting. I sort of fell in the spring!" She laughed rather weakly and noticed that neither of the young men had cracked a smile.

She hurried over to Chieftain to mount, but Johnny was at her side by the time she got there.

"Up you go!" He laughed and held her stirrup so she could put her foot into it and swing into her saddle easily.

But when she was in the saddle and turned to call good-bye to Stan, he wasn't there. He had disappeared into the brush.

Annette was disappointed. She had wanted to tell him that she hoped she'd see him again soon.

Johnny saw her expression and said teasingly, "Sorry if I interrupted a romance, chick!"

Annette's chin went up. "You didn't," she said coolly. Johnny swung into his saddle as Annette started Chieftain up the trail.

"That's good! You had me worried there, for a minute!" Johnny called after her lightly.

But Annette slapped the reins against Chieftain's neck and rode on without answering. She had met other good-looking young men with a line like Johnny's, and she had no intention of encouraging him to turn on the charm. Especially as he was Tonia's favorite character just now!

# 6       *Mystery at Morgan Hill*

Annette and Johnny had very little to say to each other as they rode the widening trail that led to the deserted gold town of Morgan Hill.

At first, Johnny tried to tease her a little more about Stan Turner, but Annette cut him off abruptly with "Please, let's find something else to talk about." Her cool dignity was discouraging, and Johnny sulked for the rest of the ride. He even rode a few yards ahead of her to show his indifference to the pretty, dark-haired girl.

But Annette didn't mind his silence. She was thinking about Stan Turner and his unfortunate father. She decided that she'd ask her uncle to do something to help Stan find the missing prospector, even though the judge was apparently convinced that there wasn't a chance of finding him alive.

The rest of the riders were waiting for them in what had once been the center of the old town. Ailanthus trees grew along the winding Main Street that had been named Sailor Gulch, the location of the first claims. Chinese miners had planted those "trees of heaven" as tiny slips that they had brought from their faraway country. Those trees, now so wide branching that they met in a thick tangle above the narrow street, had been the only reminder of their homeland that thousands of hard-laboring, homesick Chinese had enjoyed in the new land.

Tonia and the others had tied their horses to the long hitch rail in front of the old red brick Wells Fargo office that was now a museum of gold-rush relics. They were sitting on the worn steps, talking to a bewhiskered individual who had appeared from nowhere to offer information and guidance.

As Johnny and Annette rode up, Tonia's blue eyes quickly searched their faces. When she saw that Johnny was leaving Annette to dismount without any help from him, she couldn't help feeling relieved. He had been suspiciously eager to ride back to see what was delaying her cousin. Apparently, Tonia had misjudged him.

"Goodness! We thought you were lost, Annette!" she exclaimed, as Annette and Johnny sat down with them.

Annette shrugged it off. "Chieftain's to blame. He picked up a pebble. Didn't Lola tell you?"

"Sure, I did!" Tomboyish Lola grinned. "I told Johnny he didn't have to go to the rescue. But he *would* be a hero!" She looked at Johnny mockingly. "Did-ums have to rescue the lovely princess from a mean ol' dragon?"

Everyone but Johnny laughed, and he scowled. When they had quieted down, he said sarcastically, "Not a full-sized one. Just a part-time busboy from the Malt Shop!"

Startled, they all looked at Annette, and as she colored painfully and glared at Johnny, they all laughed again and Johnny smirked at her.

"Hey, what's going on?" Deke grinned and shook a finger at Annette. "Come on, confess!"

"Annette! You didn't tell me you had a date!" Tonia said with a giggle.

"And blaming it on her poor old hoss!" added Tim, shaking his head.

Annette jumped to her feet and stood looking at them defiantly. "I just happened to meet a friend while I was resting Chieftain and getting a drink of water." She gave

Johnny a withering look that made him squirm. "And if you'd like to know his name, it's Stanley Turner. And he's a very nice person."

They all looked abashed except Johnny. He snorted impolitely but didn't speak.

"Gosh, Annette," Deke said hastily, "I didn't mean to needle you."

"Me neither!" Tim chimed in.

Tonia rose hastily and put her arm around Annette's waist. "Don't mind Johnny! He's always teasing!" She threw a playfully reproachful look at the tall, good-looking blond boy. "Let's go look at the old account books in here! Wait till you see the prices people had to pay for things!"

They all trooped inside, with the local guide leading the way, and spent the next half hour examining the yellowed pages of the ancient account books with their old-fashioned Spencerian handwriting and their amazing figures.

"Sugar, three dollars a pound; molasses, five dollars a gallon; flour, a dollar and a half a pound; sardines, four dollars a can," Annette read from the grocery store records. "No wonder a lot of them came out without a fortune!"

"You folks care to see the inside of the hotel?" the local whiskered fellow inquired.

"Not much chance!" Deke squinted regretfully at the barred iron door and the iron shutters closed tight.

"Could be arranged," Whiskers suggested, dangling a brass key.

Johnny laughed, digging down into his pocket for a silver dollar. "Here! Use that for a key!"

The older man caught it deftly, and after weighing it critically in his hand, slipped it into his pocket. "Thanks, sonny," he said. "Come on in, an' don't mind the dust."

The door opened easily, without the rusty squeak that they had expected, and their guide pressed a button that flooded the lobby with a glare of electricity.

They blinked, astonished. Whiskers chuckled. "Piped it in when the high lines were strung through the gulch. Figgered it was safer than coal oil and folks could see more. Soon as the doin's start at Lost Creek, we're countin' on a coupla hundred a day to drop in."

The place was shabby and crowded with relics of gold rush days. And there was dust everywhere, dulling the gilt of the ornate mirror frames that hung over the spindly-legged tables, their stiff bouquets of wax flowers under bell-shaped glass covers.

There was a large framed picture of President Ulysses S. Grant, and one of Henry Ward Beecher, on the wall behind a horsehair sofa that looked like a twin of the one in Annette's room at the Bori home. There was a dusty ribbon stretched across it to keep visitors from sitting on it, and a stern sign warned, KEEP OFF.

Tonia and Johnny turned the pages of the hotel register and exclaimed excitedly at the names they found.

"John Jacob Astor, Junior! Mark Twain! Bret Harte!" they read out. "Lola Montez! And Lotta Crabtree!"

Johnny turned suddenly as someone tapped him on the shoulder. It was the whiskered one. "If you folks are figgerin' to take pictures up at the mine, like you was talkin' a mite ago, you better get started. Sun goes down in a coupla hours."

"Oh, I'm glad you reminded us!" Tonia grabbed Johnny's arm. "It's about five minutes' ride to the Big Mine. C'mon, everybody! Pictures!"

The tired gray buildings of the mine that had paid its owners millions in gold ore so many years ago stood on a bleak hillside without even a tree to shade them from the brilliant Sierra sunshine. Gaping holes in the rocky hill showed where the ore cars had gone in for their loads, but there were wire fences to keep out the curious now. Some of the shafts were a mile deep, and the old buckets, in which the men had descended to their backbreaking labor in the heart of the hill, now lay broken and splintered in tangles of rotting ropes and rusty cables.

A high-sided ore wagon stood apart on its tall iron-bound wheels, and a rusty old locomotive with a flared smokestack made a good background for Deke's and Tim's snapshots of the group.

It was all very picturesque and exciting, but it took the combined arguments of all the others to convince Deke that it would be foolhardy for him to climb the heavy wire fence just to get a closer shot of an old rusty wheelbarrow lying in a colorful patch of yellow California poppies and purple wild peas at the mouth of one of the mine shafts.

"Okay," he sighed finally, "but it would have been a gasser!" And he trudged off to what looked like a narrow footpath circling the hill. He went out of sight on it, looking for more scenery to photograph.

"I hope Deke doesn't go too far away." Tonia frowned. "We should be starting home soon."

But just as she finished speaking, they heard Deke calling excitedly, "Hey! I found something!" And a moment later, he came into view around the side of the hill, carrying a small object in his hand and waving it excitedly at them.

Johnny and Tim started off at once, all excitement, and the girls weren't far behind.

"Maybe it's gold ore!" Lola exclaimed as they ran after the boys.

When they got to the spot where Johnny and Tim were examining the thing that Deke had found, all three were disappointed to see that it was a pipe—an ordinary corncob pipe like the ones that the Lost Creek grocery man had put in stock for the tourists to buy as souvenirs.

"Ugh!" Tonia said disgustedly. "A smelly old pipe!"

"It's a souvenir!" Deke grinned. And he bent over and tapped the pipe on a rock so the old ashes would fall out. "I picked it up over by those rocks, and there were boot marks near it. Somebody else has been poking around here since the rain."

For a moment, Annette thought that it might have been Stan Turner. Then she realized that he couldn't have come up Morgan Hill on foot so quickly and without one of them having seen him. So she didn't mention him. There had been enough talk about Stan anyhow! And, besides, he didn't seem like the pipe-smoking type.

Johnny nudged Deke suddenly and pointed to the ground where Deke had knocked out the burned tobacco. "Look!" A tiny spiral of smoke was rising from a few blades of dry grass. "Those were live coals!"

"Hey," Tim told Deke, "better put that pipe back where you found it. The owner's still around!"

"Gosh! And I thought it was just hot from lying in the sun!" Deke scanned the hillside but couldn't see anyone.

"You're lucky you didn't get shot! Stealing souvenirs!" Tim razzed him.

"I'm putting it back right now!" Deke declared and started off, holding the pipe gingerly in his fingers. They strolled after him, laughing, but they were still at quite a distance when he carefully set the pipe down in a sunny spot and turned to hurry back to them.

It was just then that he heard a small sound, high above him, on the ridge. He shaded his eyes, staring up. It had sounded like metal striking rock.

He was just in time to see a boulder detach itself from the rimrock and start to fall. He caught a brief flash of movement where the heavy chunk of rock had been. He wasn't sure if it was only his imagination, but he thought, for a second, that the figure of a man had stood there, looking down, before disappearing.

As Deke stared hard, trying to make out that figure again, the boulder's first low, lazy bounces turned into high leaps as it picked up speed. It was coming down directly at him, bringing with it a growing shower of rocks and pebbles of all sizes. He stood watching it come. He wanted to run, to get away. But he was frozen with fear.

"This way, Deke!" Johnny yelled.

"Look out!" Tim shouted.

Lola and Tonia were screaming, "Deke! Hurry!" And when it seemed that Deke was about to be engulfed, Tonia covered her face with her hands and burst into hysterical sobs. Annette watched hopelessly, her eyes wide with shock.

But somehow, at the last possible moment, Deke found his legs and started to run back along the hillside trail. He had almost cleared the path of the avalanche when it came roaring down. The big boulder bounded by so close that he felt the breeze stir his hair, and a second afterward a shower of stinging sand, pebbles, and small rocks nearly swept him down the hill. Somehow, he kept his feet on the narrow path, and a moment later he was safe beyond the edge of the rockfall.

"Boy! That was close!" He gasped as he ran up to them and grabbed Tim's arm to steady himself. "And all over a two-bit pipe!" He was dusty from head to foot, and his face had been cut by a sharp-edged chunk of rock.

"Hey! You mean some crazy man sent those rocks down on purpose?" Tim demanded, glaring up at the empty ridge.

"I dunno!" Deke frowned. "I heard hammering, and when I took a gander up there, the rocks were coming down. And I *think* I saw a guy. I wouldn't bet on it."

They all scanned the ridge, but there was no sign of life there.

"Aw!" Johnny waved it aside grandly. "It was probably a natural slide, what with all the rain we've had around here."

"Sure! Johnny's right, I bet!" Tim assured his pal.

Deke nodded with a grin. "I guess it was the sun in my eyes that made me think I saw somebody up there." But he looked up again for a moment, not quite convinced. He could see nothing but rock shadows.

"Let's go home!" Tonia, with Lola's arm around her, was still shaking a little, and her cheeks were still damp with tears. "It's spooky!"

"Okay, chick! Let's cut out!" Johnny grinned. He took Tonia's hand and started to run with her toward the horses. At first she held back, protesting, but as he laughed and drew her along, she began giggling happily and running with him, blond ponytail waving behind.

Deke and Tim were putting away their camera equipment when Lola and Annette started down the hill, side by side.

"Do you think somebody started that slide?" Lola asked. "I don't. I think Deke is just being dramatic! I think it was probably the mine caretaker who left his pipe where Deke found it. He's probably staying out of sight so we tourists won't pester him to get past the wire fences to take our silly pictures."

Annette hesitated a moment. She was tempted to tell Lola that her guess was wrong. Because there *had* been a man up there on the ridge!

Annette had seen him when she'd looked up quickly to see what had caused the sound. The others hadn't paid any attention, so they had missed seeing the man. But she had gotten a good look at him.

He had turned away as the boulder broke loose and started downward. Annette had seen that he was wearing a full black beard and a slouch hat, and was stockily built. He had shouldered a pickax and jumped out of sight, probably down the far side of the hill.

It probably *had* been the caretaker, as Johnny guessed, and he probably hadn't intended to hurt Deke—just to scare them all away. There was no use telling the others that she had seen the man, Annette decided. Johnny, the showboat, would want to start something. And that burly man looked, even at a glance, like somebody who'd be too rough for any of the three boys to tangle with!

So she just smiled and told Lola, "You could be right!" And they followed Tonia and Johnny to get their horses and head back to Lost Creek.

Days later, she would wish that she had spoken out!

# 7 *Crosscurrents*

"Two more days before the celebration really starts!" Tonia smiled across the breakfast table at her cousin. "I can hardly wait. I adore wearing costumes!"

"So do I!" Annette admitted. "And especially the sort Aunt Betta and you brought down from the city for me to wear! I haven't tried them on yet, but they look simply stunning!"

"They're real, you know. Mom's grandmother brought several of them on a sailing ship around the Horn in 1852. In her diary she tells of wearing the blue pompadour silk for her wedding dress. And Mom is letting me wear it to the square dance, the big night of the celebration." Tonia smiled mysteriously, as if she knew some secret that she couldn't share.

But Annette knew what it was. Tonia had been hinting that there was a very good chance that the committee would consider it appropriate to choose Judge Bori's daughter to reign as queen over the centennial celebration. Theirs was one of the oldest families in El Dorado County.

"It should look good with the queen's crown!" Annette assured her, with a twinkle in her eye.

"Oh, do you really think I'll be chosen?" Tonia looked innocently hopeful.

"They're goofy if they pick anybody else!" Annette said and meant it.

"That's what Johnny says!" Tonia admitted, fluttering her lashes modestly. "And, of course, after he wins the singing contest, he can be Prince Charming and lead the grand march with me."

"It sounds like a neat arrangement." Annette smiled. "But suppose somebody else wins the singing contest? Won't you have to choose the winner to be your prince?"

"I told you," Tonia said blandly, "Johnny's the best. You just don't appreciate him."

Annette smiled. Maybe she *was* a little too critical of Johnny Abbott in some ways. But, just the same, she was convinced that Stan Turner's voice—as she had heard it, without any accompaniment except little Margie's off-key harmonica playing—had sounded two hundred percent better. It was just possible that Tonia and her friend Johnny might be due for a surprise.

Katey came in to clear off the table. "You two better get a move on if you're goin' to the dressmaker's with Miz' Bori. She's out front in her car."

"Oops! I forgot!" Tonia jumped up and pushed her chair back. "Thanks, Katey. Come on, Annette."

"What are we going to a dressmaker for?"

"Wait till you try to squeeze into one of those silk and lace numbers of Great Granny's! Those gals wore iron cages that pinched 'em in the middle and bulged them out at the top!"

"Heavens! Do we have to wear those thingamabobs?"

"They're not getting me into one!" Tonia announced as they went dashing outside and down the steep porch steps to the waiting car. "I like breathing!"

"First a fitting," Aunt Betta announced. "Then I'll buy you two some lunch, if the town isn't too mobbed with tourists."

The tourists *were* pouring in, and the town was taking on its yearly briskness. The storekeepers all wore smiling faces behind their beards, and the lady clerks suffered in tight-fitting gingham wrappers and high-buttoned shoes. But the cash registers were starting to sing a happy song, and the hotel registers were filling up with names.

The little dressmaker in her side-street home was wide-eyed with admiration as Mrs. Bori spread out the rich silk dresses on her table.

"This pale blue pompadour silk for Tonia," she agreed, nodding vigorously. "And the white with ruffles for Miss Annette. Perfect!"

The fitting was quick and painless, except for a few stifled yelps as the dressmaker tried to fasten some strategic hooks and eyes and failed by several inches.

"Will it be ready for Saturday night?" Tonia asked, as she shook herself out of the blue silk with the dressmaker's help.

"The sewing will be done," the seamstress promised, "but my advice to you is no malted milks or hot fudge sundaes all week!"

"Oh, pooh!" Tonia frowned. "Everybody'll think I'm a drip when we go to the Malt Shop."

"Of course, if you'd rather wear your old pink strapless, with my paisley shawl and a sunbonnet," Mrs. Bori suggested teasingly. "At least you wouldn't be in danger of bursting out a seam!"

"Oh, okay!" Tonia pouted. "We'll drink buttermilk, won't we, Annette?"

"I adore it!" Annette agreed, wrinkling her nose and making a funny face that started them all laughing.

But a few minutes later, when they found a table in the Star Lunchroom, both girls were careful to order buttermilk, cottage cheese salad with fresh vegetables, and melba toast. And only Mrs. Bori ordered the Lunchroom's special cream pie for dessert and enjoyed it in spite of two pairs of hungry eyes watching every mouthful.

It was only when the slim, sad-faced waitress brought their check that Annette looked closely at her and thought she reminded her of someone. And then, when Mrs. Bori said, "Thank you, Mrs. Turner. The lunch was very good!" Annette realized suddenly why she had seemed familiar. She was Stan and Margie's mother! Annette had forgotten that Margie had said she worked there.

A few minutes later, as Mrs. Bori and Tonia went ahead toward the door, Annette stopped impulsively to speak to Mrs. Turner. "I'm Annette McCleod. I guess Margie told you about my having a flat tire the other night near your house"—she hesitated shyly, but the pleasant smile that lit up Mrs. Turner's face encouraged her to finish— "so I'm very glad to have met you."

"It's good to know you, too. The kids told me," she said, nodding, still with the smile, and turning to clear the table. "You made a hit with Margie," she added over her shoulder.

Annette hurried out after her aunt and Tonia, feeling a pleasant warmth. She hadn't been disappointed in Stan and Margie's mother. She was a friendly person.

Tonia was alone. Mrs. Bori had gone on another errand that didn't concern the girls. "What on earth were you and the waitress talking about?" she asked.

"Why—she's Stan Turner's mother," Annette explained. "I was just saying hello."

"That's funny. I didn't know she was *that* Mrs. Turner. She looks awfully sad. I guess it's natural." Then she changed the subject lightly. "Let's go buy some silly souvenirs and make believe we're tourists."

So they spent the next couple of hours browsing in what the local newspaper playfully called "tourist traps" and buying all sorts of silly things. Most of them came from far-distant countries to catch the pennies of the unwary shopper who, not bothering to look at the label on the bottom of his "genuine souvenir of the Mother Lode," would be just as happy with it when he got it home as if it had been authentic. After all, labels were easily removed!

It was when they started home at last, laden with knick-knacks, that Tonia spied Johnny coming out of the express office with a bulky, well-wrapped box. His convertible was at the curb, its top down as usual.

"Hi!" Tonia wasn't above calling across the street when she wanted to attract someone's attention. "Taxi!"

"Sugar!" Johnny seemed very pleased to see them. "Come on over and I'll drive you dolls home!"

They waited for the green light and then dashed across, while Johnny was stowing away the large package in his car trunk and closing the lid.

Tonia was curious. "Looks like Santa Claus was early!" she hinted, nodding toward the closed trunk.

Johnny smiled broadly. It was that same pleased, self-satisfied smirk that irritated Annette each time she met him. "What'll you give me for telling you what's in there?" he teased.

Tonia blushed prettily and tossed her ponytail. "Maybe I don't want to know!"

"Okay! Suffer till I get ready to tell you then!" He laughed as he opened the car door and waved them in. "Climb aboard and I'll tell you a keen idea for tomorrow. That is, if you two chicks aren't tied up?"

"Oh, no! We were just wondering what to do!" Tonia answered hopefully as she settled in the middle of the seat and made room for Annette on the outside.

"Well, I just saw Lola, and she said something about a picnic on the river and some nugget hunting."

"She and I were talking about it yesterday," Annette said eagerly. "We thought it would be fun!"

"Let's do it!" Tonia agreed heartily. "Mom knows the spot where she and Dad found some nuggets last year. I'll ask her to take us!"

"Swell!" Johnny grinned, getting behind the wheel. "You kids make the arrangements."

"I'll call the gang the minute we get home!" Tonia said happily. "We can wear old-timer things over our bathing suits and pretend we're pioneers!"

"And I'll bring my guitar and we'll practice 'Juanita' and a couple of others that I've dug up for us to duet on! Hey, Annette?"

"Whatever the rest want to do." Annette shrugged.

"How about having a wienie roast for lunch?" Tonia was still making happy plans.

"A real gold-town blast!" Johnny agreed, in an unusually happy mood. He started the convertible off from the curb, just missing a delivery truck, and roared up the street.

Showing off as usual! Annette thought, and closed her eyes tight as Johnny made a quick turn up into the side street that led to the Bori home, his hopped-up motor roaring.

He made a fast stop with squealing brakes in front of the tall white mansion, bringing scared shrieks from both girls, who nearly hit the windshield.

Annette's knees were shaking as she got out of the big car. I'd like to bawl him out, she thought angrily. But she swallowed her words because Tonia was smiling up into the big goof's face and telling him how sweet it was of him to give them a lift.

He left them at the steps and roared off down the hill with full power on.

Tonia started up the steps and then noticed that Annette was holding one hand cupped behind her ear, listening expectantly for something.

"What on earth?" Tonia asked, puzzled.

"The crash. He missed twice coming up. He's due to smack into something the third time!" Annette was half in earnest.

"Sill-ee-e!" Tonia giggled. "Johnny's a sharp driver! He never gets into trouble!"

"I bet the local law just loves him!" Annette ran up the steps and they hurried inside, heading straight for the phone.

Mrs. Bori heard their plans for the picnic with interest. "Good! All six of you can ride in the station wagon with me. I've been wanting to see that spot along the creek again. It's just the right time of year, while snow water's coming down. There's a chance of finding a nugget that's been washed out of some pocket in the High Sierra. Dad and I found a couple last year."

They were off to an early start the next morning. Again, it was Lola, Tim, and Deke who went with the girls and Johnny Abbott.

They all wore bathing suits underneath their pioneer outfits. Johnny looked quite handsome in well-fitted, homespun trousers tucked into miner's boots and topped by a handsome plaid shirt. Deke and Tim settled for dungarees and T-shirts under Army surplus jackets. They had fun razzing Johnny for his "pretty" outfit, but no amount of teasing would make him tell what was in the somewhat bulky bundle that he stowed away under his seat in the station wagon, along with his guitar.

"You'll find out," he assured them lazily as they waited for the girls to join them in front of the Bori house.

Tonia and Annette came out, lugging a big picnic basket, as old Mike brought the station wagon from the garage. Tonia was in a sprigged calico skirt with a lace-trimmed white linen blouse and a saucy sunbonnet that matched the voluminous skirt.

Annette had on a "wrapper" of red bandanna cloth which set off her black hair. Her sunbonnet was of the same material, and with her darker skin and eyes, she looked as if she might have been a genuine pioneer girl, browned by the long trek overland.

Lola, who had walked up the hill with Deke and Tim, wore a "dust-catcher" skirt of brown homespun, a wide patent-leather belt, and a plaid blouse, topped by a sailor hat.

Tim and Deke hurried to relieve the girls of the picnic basket, pretending to be almost collapsing under its weight as they staggered with it to the station wagon.

All the girls laughed at their clowning, and Tonia called out, "You drop that and you don't eat!" as she ran after them, pretending to be alarmed.

As Annette picked up her trailing skirt and started to follow Tonia, she felt a hand on her arm and turned, startled, to look up into Johnny's admiring eyes.

"I've got to have a color shot of you in that outfit!" Johnny told her masterfully. "Stand over here in the sun." He swung her around and started her toward a blossom-filled Burmese honeysuckle vine at the corner of the house.

But Annette stopped before she had gone five feet and drew free of Johnny's hand on her arm. She looked past him and called to Tonia at the station wagon, "Tone! Johnny wants to take our picture!"

Tonia turned and came running back, happily excited. "Wait till I get the shine off my nose!" she told Johnny as she hurried toward them.

"I said I wanted *your* picture!" Johnny frowned. But Annette met his scowl with an innocent look of surprise, and he had to wipe off the frown as Tonia ran up, ready to pose her prettiest.

He took one exposure of their pretty faces against the honeysuckle blossoms and then said, "Now, you alone this time, Annette." He waved Tonia aside.

But Annette had seen Mrs. Bori and the judge coming out the front door, and she picked up her skirts and ran toward them, brushing Johnny's detaining hand aside. He glared after her, ignoring Tonia. "Annette!" he called crossly. "I'm ready to shoot!"

"How's this pose?" Tonia drew a heavy spray of honeysuckle down beside her pink cheeks and smiled at Johnny. But he was still frowning after Annette.

Without attempting to take Tonia's picture, he started putting away his camera. She stared at him in surprise. "What's the matter?"

"No more film. That was the last of the roll!" he told her abruptly. "I'll reload when we get to the creek. Come on! Looks like everybody's ready to go."

He took her arm and led her toward the station wagon where the judge was giving explicit last-minute directions to his wife on how to find the spot where they had picked up nuggets last year. Mrs. Bori listened politely, but since she had been the driver last year, she felt that she might be able to find it without too much trouble *this* year!

Then it was "all aboard" and away they all went, with much laughter and expectation of a happy day.

But Johnny was moody and had little to say. And Annette felt just a little ashamed of the way she had snubbed him, even though it had been for Tonia's sake.

Maybe I'd better be a little friendlier with him, she thought, and keep him from putting a wet blanket on the party, the creep! So she looked back gaily at him from her seat beside Aunt Betta. "Get out the guitar, why don't you, Johnny?" she called. "Let's do some harmonizing!"

And it seemed to work. Johnny whipped out the guitar, and they were soon all singing together.

Tonia joined in, but she wasn't happy. She was wondering why Johnny hadn't noticed that he was out of film when he asked Annette to pose—but he knew it without checking the camera when *she* was ready to let him take *her* picture!

# 8        *The Nugget*

The picnic spot on the bank of the creek was only a mile and a half from town, but because the road was narrow and unmarked, no camper had found his way to it so far this summer. Which meant that its manzanita thicket and the willows at the water's edge had no tin can decorations and the young grass at the foot of its tall oaks was free of banana skins and orange peels.

Mrs. Bori turned off the dirt road and parked the station wagon in a shady spot, sheltered from the brisk wind that was blowing up whitecaps on the swift-moving creek. "The creek looks pretty high, and I imagine it's too cold for swimming," she advised them as the six started piling out of the car.

"I'll take your word for it, Mrs. Bori," Deke said.

But Johnny, unloading his mysterious bundle from under the seat, merely smiled to himself. He strode over to the brush with the package and disappeared for a moment. When he came in sight again, he was empty-handed, but still wearing a knowing smile.

Mrs. Bori had brought several skillets from the kitchen and a couple of shallow, old-fashioned tin washbasins from the judge's collection of antiques. She handed the heavier pans to the boys, the tin basins to the girls. "The best place to look should be at the roots of those willows right along the bank," she told them. "The creek drops a foot or more there, and you may find some gold flakes caught in the roots."

"Nuggets or nothin'!" Tim declared, flourishing the short-handled shovel he had brought for digging.

"You'll have to dig deeper for a nugget," Mrs. Bori pointed out. "Gold is a lot heavier than gravel, and a nugget sinks pretty soon after it's washed down by the current."

"Same as sand crabs at the ocean!" Deke put in.

"Well, more or less!" Tonia's mother laughed.

"Come on, everybody!" Johnny was starting off, shovel over his shoulder, frying pan in hand.

Tim and Deke followed him, clowning a conga line. And Lola fell in line behind them. But Annette noticed that her cousin was standing aside, a pout on her pretty face.

"Coming, Tone? Let's show up these characters and dig up a whopper of a nugget!" she called cheerfully.

But Tonia waved her on. "I'll be along," she answered. "Go ahead."

Annette hurried after Lola and the boys, stumbling a little over her long skirts as she ran across the grass, flourishing her tin pan and the buffalo-horn spoon that was also part of the judge's collection. Many a spoonful of gravel had been dug by that ancient relic, but it was still sturdy and ready for another hundred years of use.

Halfway to the water's edge, Johnny and his conga line had broken into song, and Annette joined in as she fell in behind Lola:

"In a cavern, in a canyon, excavating for a mine,
Lived a miner, forty-niner, and his daughter
    Clementine!"

they sang happily.

"Dear, aren't you going to do some panning, too?" Mrs. Bori was puzzled at Tonia's hesitation.

Tonia's voice was cool, but her eyes were stormy with anger and hurt feelings. "Heavens, no! I'm not putting *my* hands into that ice water! I'm too chilly now."

"Let me get you some hot chocolate, dear. There's a full thermos." Mrs. Bori was worried. It wasn't like Tonia to sulk, but apparently something had gone wrong.

"Oh, stop fussing, Mother! If I want a hot drink, I know where to get it! Just leave me alone." She turned away abruptly and went to sit on a sun-drenched rock from which she could watch the others as they lined up along the bank with their pans and shovels and prepared to start the nugget hunt.

Mrs. Bori sighed and went back to the car to read. I wonder what age they have to be before you can understand them, she thought with a shake of her head.

Tonia frowned as she watched Johnny show Lola how to tip up the gravel in her tin basin and rock it gently under the flowing water so the sand and bits of rock would wash out and leave the gold flakes, if there were any. Yesterday, Tonia thought angrily, he said he and I would do our panning together today. And now he acts as if he doesn't even notice that I'm not there!

A few minutes later, when Johnny strolled up to

see what was wrong, she managed to smile coolly at him.

"What's the lonesome bit for, doll?" he asked, lazily smiling. He took hold of her chin and lifted it so that she'd have to look him in the eyes. "Mad at somebody?"

"Of course not!" Tonia's eyes flashed. "I just don't feel like that silly kid stuff."

"Oh, come along, chick! Old Johnny'll find you a nice shiny hunk of gold!" He caught her hand and drew her to her feet.

Tonia pulled free. "Give it to Lola—or Annette!" And she picked up her long skirt and marched away toward the car.

Johnny scowled after her—"Okay, if that's the way you feel!"—and he wheeled and stamped down to the water's edge again.

"Where's Tonia?" Annette called over to him from where she was squatting on the creek bank, rocking the gravel in her basin. The water was cold and she had found nothing.

"I think she has a headache or somethin'," he said indifferently. "She doesn't want to do any panning."

"She's got more brains than we have!" Lola said disgustedly, standing up and flipping her empty basin aside.

"If there ever was any gold around here, Clementine must've dug it out when she and her pappy were here!"

Deke groaned and held his aching back as he stood up. "I quit! I'll buy my nuggets in the jewelry store!"

"Weaklings!" Annette teased them. "I came to get a nugget, and I'm not giving up till I get one!" And she went back to her tin basin.

"I'm with you!" Tim declared. "Shoo, the rest of you! Don't scare our nuggets away!" He waved the others away and squatted down beside Annette. "Carry on, stout feller!"

"Good lad!" she said gravely. "Cheerio!"

"Pip-pip!" Tim replied, and they dipped out more gravel. "Join us, old chap!" he called to Johnny.

But Johnny had started for the thicket where he had left his bundle, and now he went out of sight.

"Now what has Handsome got up his well-tailored shirtsleeve?" Lola wondered to Deke.

"Who cares?" Deke grinned, and they sauntered up to join Tonia on the sunny rock.

By the time Johnny appeared again, a few minutes later, Tim and Annette had also given up their panning, because their fingers were half frozen.

They threw themselves down on the grass near Tonia's rock and let the sun hit their icy hands. "Br-r-r!" Tim shivered. "The Eskimos can have—" He broke off abruptly, staring. "Hey! Look at Superman!"

They all looked. It was Johnny in bathing trunks—wearing a skin-diving mask, tank, and swim fins. He went up the creek to where the bank was higher above the water and free of willows.

Tim and Deke exchanged looks. "Wouldn't you know it?" Tim whispered out of the side of his mouth. "The show-off!"

Johnny paused on the edge of the bank and turned to wave to them. Then he leaped, feetfirst, into the stream.

Tonia jumped up and started to run to where she could watch him, and Annette and Lola were close on her heels. But Tim and Deke just sat and sunned themselves lazily.

"I hope he knows what he's doing!" Lola exclaimed.

"Isn't he daring?" Tonia pulled at Annette's sleeve.

Annette looked at the fast-moving current and frowned, shaking her head disapprovingly. "I think he's being silly. The boys I know down home never go skin-diving alone. They have too much sense. They use the buddy system."

Tonia was too intent on Johnny's bobbing head to pay

any attention to what Annette was saying. Johnny was well out in the center of the creek now, swimming strongly.

Lola looked worried. "Buddy system?"

"They dive in pairs, with a buddy," Annette explained. "That way, if one gets into any kind of trouble, the other is right there to help. It has saved a lot of swimmers' lives."

Lola nodded understandingly. "Let's keep our fingers crossed!"

Tonia tossed her ponytail. "Johnny can take care of himself. He's strong—and smart, too!"

Annette shrugged. Why argue when Tonia apparently had no idea how dangerous white water like that could be?

Suddenly, Johnny was out of sight, under the water. And it seemed to all of them that it was ages before he came popping up again, close to the bank.

"Thank goodness!" Lola said. "Heaven takes care of stupes like him!"

Johnny was wading ashore, now, down where they had been panning for gold. He pulled off his face mask and waved to them. "I found a dinger! Look!" He splashed awkwardly up onto the bank, holding out something in his hand. It shone in the sunlight, a water-smoothed nugget of gold, a little smaller than a sparrow's egg.

Mrs. Bori, watching tensely from the station wagon, gave a sigh of relief at the sight of Johnny and went back to her reading.

Deke and Tim ran down hastily to see what Johnny had found, and Johnny swaggered a bit as he laid the shining pebble on Deke's palm. "Take a hinge at *that*, bud!"

"Phew! It must be worth five bucks!" Deke hefted it and then started to bite into it.

Johnny retrieved it quickly. "It's the real McCoy. You don't have to chew any chunks off it to find out!" And, ignoring Tonia, he turned to Annette, the nugget held up between his thumb and finger. "Pretty neat, hey? Bet it would look good on a neck chain!"

"I suppose so," Annette agreed casually. Then, as she turned away, she said to Lola, "I'm starved. Let's ask Aunt Betta if we can help get lunch." She thought Johnny would want to make a ceremony of presenting the nugget to Tonia. The rest of them might be in the way. "Come on, boys. You can help, too!"

But as she started past Johnny, he reached out and caught hold of her hand. "Wait! It's for you. Take it," he said, as he held out the nugget to her.

Tonia stiffened and stared, shocked, and Annette was

too surprised for a moment to react. The others looked at each other questioningly.

Then Annette frowned and pulled her hand away from Johnny's. "No, thanks, Johnny. I don't have a chain anyhow."

"That's easy to take care of," Johnny went on boldly. "Come on! Take it. I got the thing just for you. You can't turn it down."

There was a moment of heavy silence. Deke and Tim let their eyes flick to Tonia's white face, and Lola stared disgustedly at Johnny.

"Sorry," Annette said carelessly, "but I've got all the junk jewelry I need now!" She turned her back to Johnny deliberately, linked her arm with Lola's, and they started back toward the car together.

"Good show, kid!" Lola said the moment they were out of earshot. "That set Casanova back on his haunches!"

"I didn't mean to be snippy," Annette said soberly. "I guess I was pretty mean, but he's a big nothing so far as I'm concerned, even if Tonia thinks he's a livin' doll."

Johnny, red-faced, glared after Annette. There was a snicker from Deke, and Johnny glowered at him threateningly. Deke looked innocent. Johnny's temper was nothing to fool with, and he was a lot bigger than Deke or Tim.

Tonia still stood looking at Johnny with a hurt expression, tears welling up in her eyes.

"You said you wouldn't want it! Here! Take it!" He thrust the nugget into her hand and closed her fingers around it. "You can have it!"

Tonia stepped back, her face flushed with anger, and flung the tiny chunk of gold as far into the brush as she could. Then she told him furiously, "I don't want it, thanks! I can get my own nugget if I want one!" Then she wheeled around quickly and marched away toward the car, head high.

"Boy, are you popular with the femmes!" Tim chortled.

For once, Johnny had no ready answer. He ripped off the swim fins and dumped the mask and the tank with them in a heap on the ground. He was furious as he disappeared into the brush.

"Gosh!" Tim said. "What happens now?"

Deke waved carelessly. "They'll make up before lunch!"

But a lot more was to happen before they did.

# 9        *A Narrow Escape*

Tonia's mother was glad to have the girls helping her get the lunch spread out on the portable picnic table under the oaks. Usually, stopping to eat was the last thing they wanted to do when they were enjoying themselves.

There must be something wrong today, she thought. They're all being too quiet and too polite to one another—especially the girls.

Tim and Deke had brought the small iron hibachi from the car and were lighting the coals in it to broil the frankfurters. They were doing a lot of puffing and blowing to get the fire started, and arguing about how the Japanese would have done it in their own country. Of course, neither of them had ever been to Japan—or read the directions that had come with the small firepot! But their argument furnished the only live spot at the picnic.

Tonia was spreading the bright plastic cover on the picnic table. Johnny came up and tried to talk to her. But it was evident to everyone there that she was snubbing him, because Johnny suddenly stalked away and went to sit by himself with his back turned, plunking away on his guitar.

Lola set the bowl of salad on the table and stood back to admire it, as Tonia laid out the serving spoons and the plastic forks and butter spreaders.

"Your mom certainly can whip up a gorgeous mess of salad!" Lola helped herself to a mammoth ripe olive. "Mmm, yum! Aren't you just starved?"

"Not particularly," Tonia answered and went back to the car for plates and napkins.

Lola looked after her, head cocked to one side. Then she strolled over to Annette, who had drawn the job of cutting Katey's three-layer coconut cake into generous slices.

"Can't we get those two lovebirds to make up and start cooing again?" she asked abruptly. "All this fun and frolic is wearing me out!"

Annette looked at Johnny, off to one side with his

guitar. Then she glanced at Tonia, pouting, but casting occasional glances toward Johnny as if she hoped he'd try again to make up with her.

"Poor Tonia!" she said softly. "I hope I never get that goofy over anybody!"

"Especially a spoiled brat like J. Abbott!" Lola added dryly.

Annette made up her mind. She covered the cut cake with a mosquito-net umbrella and left Lola to guard it from Deke and Tim while she strolled up to the station wagon to talk to her cousin.

Tonia was folding paper napkins into little boat shapes, pretending that she didn't see Annette coming.

"Hi!" Annette said casually. "Say, those are cuties! Show me how you do it!"

Tonia crumpled up the one she had been folding and threw it away. "It's just kid stuff." And she started to walk away.

"Tonia! Wait a minute!" Annette had had just about enough pouting. "I want to talk to you."

Tonia stopped and looked back defiantly. "There's nothing to talk about."

Annette's dark eyes flashed. "Oh, yes, there is, too! You

know Johnny didn't go after that nugget for *me*, no matter what he said."

"He handed it right to you!" Tonia snapped angrily.

"But both Deke and Tim heard him remind you that you said you wouldn't want it! We all think you quarreled, and Johnny was just trying to show you he could give it to somebody else—anybody else!" She smiled. "*I* happened to be standing next to him."

Tonia looked almost convinced and she stole a quick look toward Johnny. She seemed tempted to forgive him, and Annette gave a relieved sigh. But the next moment, the pout was back on Tonia's face, and she told Annette sharply, "I don't care! I don't want his old nugget—or anyone else's! I can get one for myself if I want it!"

Annette gave up. She looked soberly at her cousin a moment, then turned and went back to Lola at the table.

"What luck?" Lola asked between crisp bites on a piece of stuffed celery. "Is everything all right again?"

"Uh-uh!" Annette looked grim as she shook her head. "I tried, but something tells me the big lug will have to do his own explaining before she'll believe what really happened with that nugget!"

Lola glanced toward Johnny and almost choked on the

celery. Johnny was on his feet now, and Mrs. Bori was smilingly taking him by the arm and coaxing him to come with her toward the two girls. He seemed to be holding back, protesting, but she was insisting pleasantly.

"Ouch!" Lola made a face. "Something tells me we're about to be entertained! I'm glad I nibbled. Once he starts performing, we'll be lucky if we eat before sunset!"

"Oh, he's not that bad!" Annette said with a grin.

Aunt Betta dragged Johnny and his guitar up to them, announcing gaily, "Johnny's been practicing the song he'll sing at the contest. It sounds charming. I want him to sing it now for all of you. We'll have a special preview!"

"I don't know it very well," Johnny protested modestly, but he swung the guitar around and strummed a couple of chords as he spoke. He wasn't going to need much coaxing!

"Deke and Tim! Stop fussing with that smoky thing for a few minutes and come listen!" Mrs. Bori called.

"This is a picnic?" Deke groaned as they started to obey the summons.

"And some people think ants are the worst that can happen!" Tim muttered. But they both managed to smile bravely as they went over to her.

"Where's Tonia?" Mrs. Bori asked after a glance back toward the station wagon, where she had last seen her daughter sitting.

The others glanced about, but there was no sign of Tonia.

"Hey!" Johnny was scowling, pointing to the spot where he had dropped his skin-diving outfit. "Who walked off with my stuff?" He glared accusingly at Deke and Tim.

But before they could indignantly deny it, they heard a halloo from the high bank from which Johnny had jumped into the creek.

Tonia, in her bathing suit and outfitted with swim fins and air tank, was waving to them. "Here I go!" she called, then pulled the mask into position on her face.

"Tonia! Wait! The water's too cold for you!" Annette was on her feet and running toward the bank. "Don't try it!"

But before Annette had gotten halfway to her, Tonia had jumped awkwardly into the water and was starting to swim with the current.

Deke and Tim were beside Annette by the time she had reached the high bank. All three could see Tonia swimming easily downstream. She looked back and saw them, gave a wave, and then swam on.

"She'll never stand that cold water!" Annette was frightened.

"Aw! Look at her go! She's doing all right!" Tim assured her. "She knows what she's doing."

"Girls can stand more cold than us guys," Deke told them. "Ask any doctor."

But Annette wasn't convinced. She ran down the bank along the edge of the water, trying to catch up with the bobbing head out in the middle of the stream. "Tonia! Tonia!" she shouted, whenever she could find breath to yell.

But Tonia was being swept along faster than Annette could fight her way through the willows on the bank. And Tonia didn't seem to be in any trouble yet, though Annette knew she would soon feel the numbing effect of the icy water.

A moment later, Tonia was carried out of sight around a bend in the stream. And before Annette followed, she glanced back and saw Johnny with Tim and Deke, watching. She saw, even at this distance, that Johnny was gesturing that there was no need to get excited.

How little he knew! River diving was far more dangerous than gliding around in the ocean. And doubly so in icy water. Anyone with brains would have worn a rubber suit to keep out the deadly cold. But not Johnny! And now Tonia—but there was no time to think about it. She had to keep Tonia in sight somehow.

Annette crashed on through the willow-grown sand at the water's edge and raced around the bend.

There was no bobbing blond head out in the middle of the stream!

Annette felt real panic for the first time. She stared at the rushing water, hoping against hope that the reflected sunlight was dazzling her eyes and that Tonia was still swimming strongly with the current.

But it was no use fooling herself. Tonia was gone. For a moment, Annette almost gave up hope. Automatically, her eyes searched the opposite bank. No sign of Tonia there.

Then she heard it! A terrified little scream that came faintly over the steady roar of the water.

She saw Tonia, five feet from the near bank, her face mask off, waving frantically with one arm, as with the other she tried to free herself from something beneath the surface of the water.

Annette was thankful in that moment that she had her bathing suit on under the hampering long skirt and tight blouse of her costume. She ripped half the buttons off the blouse getting out of it, and a moment later she was free of the skirt, too. Another minute and she had kicked off her shoes, plunged into the icy water, and, after the first gasping shock of contact, was swimming strongly toward her cousin.

Tonia's face was a mask of terror as she struggled to free herself from the tangle of old tree roots that was holding the oversized swim fin. Then she saw Annette swimming toward her, letting the current help her along. "Annette! Help me! My foot—caught . . ."

Then, as Annette got to her, Tonia fainted and started to slip under the water.

It was all Annette could do to hold Tonia's face above the water. She couldn't let go of her to try to dive down and free her cousin's foot. And she was getting more numb by the second. She wondered how long she could hold on.

Then she saw Johnny crashing along through the willows with Deke and Tim close on his heels, and far behind them, Lola and Aunt Betta.

The three boys hit the water, clothes and all, almost at the same second, but it was Johnny who reached the girls first.

"Grab her!" Annette managed to get the words out through chattering teeth and blue lips. And Johnny slipped his arm around Tonia and held her, as Annette let go and started to go under.

Deke and Tim were there before Annette could sink, and lifted her face clear of the water.

"Her foot's—caught!" she gasped.

"Okay, we'll get her loose!" Tim shouted. "Get Annette out, Deke. I'll give Johnny a hand."

By the time Deke had helped Annette reach the bank, Tim had dived and freed Tonia's foot from the tangled dead roots, and he and Johnny were bringing her to safety.

It was a quiet group that rode back toward the Bori home a little later. Annette and Tonia were well wrapped in the boys' coats and Aunt Betta's paisley shawl. Both insisted that they were feeling just fine and wished everyone wouldn't make such a fuss over them.

But Mrs. Bori was so unnerved by the near-tragedy that she turned over the driving to Johnny, and was agreeably surprised when he drove slowly and without any showing off, for a change.

Johnny was in no hurry this time. Tonia and Annette were in the front seat, and Tonia was cuddled close to him, her fingers entwined in his right hand. The ride could have gone on for hours so far as they were concerned. And Annette, noticing the signs, smiled to herself and was happy that Tonia's silly jealousy had been cured, even if it had taken something pretty close to a disaster to do it!

Now they could all be friends and settle down to having a lot of fun at the Pioneer Days celebration, which was starting tomorrow.

As the station wagon went along Main Street and passed the Malt Shop, she thought about what Johnny had called Stan Turner: a "part-time busboy from the Malt Shop."

"Maybe I'll drop in there tomorrow and find out how his little sister Margie is. She was so cute," she told herself.

And she really believed that was the main reason why she wanted to see Stan Turner again!

# 10 *Stan's Problem*

There was no sleeping late in the Bori household the next morning. It was the first day of the centennial celebration. Long before the usual time for Lost Creek's citizens to wake up and get stirring around, there were crowds of tourists arriving. And from the sound of auto horns down on Main Street, they had already managed to get into some traffic snarls.

Annette and Tonia didn't mind being awakened a bit earlier than usual. Neither of them felt any ill effects from their icy bath in the creek, and they could hardly wait to get down into the crowds and join in the fun. But first, they had to eat a good breakfast.

"What's going on today?" Aunt Betta was on so many

committees that she had given up trying to keep the program straight in her mind anymore.

Tonia helped herself to fresh cream for her cereal. "Oodles of things! Whiskerino contest, tours of the old mines and ghost towns, liars' contest! The place will be jumping!"

Mrs. Bori sighed. "Well, don't you two do too much jumping! You have a whole week ahead of you!"

The girls grinned at each other and agreed to do just that, which made Mrs. Bori feel a little relieved, but brought a secret smile from the judge as he glanced through his mail between sips of coffee. He knew that all the promises in the world wouldn't slow them down. And if there was a little sigh that followed his smile, it was because he remembered other days, when he was their age and also had no idea what it meant to "take it easy"!

"I'm finished. May we go, Mom?" Tonia pushed back from the table.

"I suppose so!" Mrs. Bori gestured helplessly.

"C'mon, Annette! Let's get into our sunbonnets!" And before her mother could think of any instructions to give them, the cousins were dashing happily out and up the stairs to put on their cotton pioneer outfits.

Judge Bori shook his head and chuckled as he looked after them. Then he sobered as he glanced through one of the messages that Katey had put beside his plate.

"What is it, dear?" Mrs. Bori asked, surprised at his serious expression.

"It's a note from Joe Patton, chairman of the Queen Committee. He says the vote was unanimous for Tonia at the meeting last night."

"Well?" Mrs. Bori couldn't understand his frown. "We expected it, didn't we? They haven't made any secret about intending to choose Tonia. Why do you look like that?"

Judge Bori sat back, swinging his reading glasses on his finger as he hesitated before answering. He knew that what he was about to say would be a shock to his wife. "I don't think Tonia should be queen. I think Annette deserves that honor."

"But why? Everyone knows Tonia! Annette is just visiting—" Mrs. Bori was bewildered.

"Yesterday Annette saved Tonia's life. I think that courage like hers should be rewarded!" He put his hand on his wife's, across the table. "Don't you, my dear?"

For a long moment, Mrs. Bori hesitated. Then, "You're

right, as usual. But"—she was, first of all, a mother—
"how will Tonia feel? You know she's been counting on
being queen. She'll be crushed."

"I know. It isn't easy for me to do, but I feel that I
should at least suggest it to Joe and his committee, in all
fairness." And as his wife continued to look unhappy, he
patted her hand. "They may not agree."

"I hope they don't!" she told him frankly. "I'm very
fond of Annette and grateful. But Tonia's my baby, and I
don't want her hurt!" She dabbed at an unwelcome tear.

Judge Bori sighed. "I think I'll walk downtown and see
Joe, before the committee issues a bulletin. Might as well
get it over with."

"Shall I say anything to the girls?" She didn't relish the
prospect.

"No. Wait. We'll see what the committee thinks." The
judge rose and walked slowly to the hall door.

But he almost changed his mind a few minutes later as
he put on his hat and picked his cane out of the hallway
umbrella stand. The two cousins, laughing gaily as they
came down the stairs arm in arm in their becoming old-
time costumes, were such a picture of happiness that he
nearly decided to let the committee's decision stand.

But Judge Bori was a man who couldn't turn back once he had chosen his course of action. He went down the hill a moment later with a pretty girl on either arm, smiling proudly as they gathered admiring glances, but inwardly feeling like a traitor.

"Let's go watch Deke and Tim build their float!" Tonia suggested as the judge left them and went on his way to the real estate office of Joe Patton on a side street.

The two boys had taken over the backyard of Deke's home and were building a replica of a miner's shack using an old wagon bed as a foundation. In the next day's Pioneer Parade, they'd both be in costume on the float. One of them would be cooking over an open fire, while the other pretended to pan for gold in a make-believe stream made of strips of aluminum foil.

"We need a pioneer female to stand in the doorway and add beauty and charm. Any takers?" Deke arched an eyebrow at Tonia and Annette. "We thought one of you—uh?"

"Flattery will get you nothing," Annette replied, "but it's the sweetest offer I've had all day. So, yes!" She smiled over at Tonia. "Tonia's going to have her own float."

Tonia dimpled and waved it away modestly. "It's not

settled yet. Goodness, nobody knows who'll be queen till the committee puts it in the *Gazette*!"

"Who else?" Tim meant it as he smiled at Tonia. "And you'll be a knockout, kid!"

"Ladies, at your service!" Johnny came strolling in, a handsome sight in a city costumer's most extravagant idea of a riverboat gambler of old Mississippi days. His drawl matched the costume as he made a courtly bow. "Gentleman Jack!"

"Johnny! How perfectly stunning!" Tonia exclaimed.

"Why, thank you, ma'am!" Johnny stayed in character. He cast an expectant look toward Annette, but she seemed unmoved. He waited a second and then decided to press the point. "How do *you* like it, Annette?" He posed.

"It's a little dressy for a gold-rush pioneer," she said frankly but with a smile. "Don't you think so, Deke?"

Johnny frowned at Deke, and Deke hurried to say, "Looks okay to me!" Then he and Tim went back to their float-building rather than get involved further.

Annette saw Johnny's sulky look starting to show. She said quickly, "But it certainly is different—and striking!"

Johnny smiled again. He swaggered a bit as he told her, "That's me, doll! Always something new!"

Oh, boy! Annette thought. How corny can he get! But she managed to keep a straight face.

Johnny went on smugly: "I have another surprise for you chicks! My dad just sent down a new electric guitar for me to use in the contest Saturday. Like to hear it this morning? I'll run you over to my place if you do, and Mom'll fix us lunch."

"We'd love it!" Tonia was delighted. But Annette was silent.

"Come along then, glamour gals!" Johnny linked his arm with Tonia's and offered the other one to Annette.

"I'm sorry," she said, "but there's something I have to tend to downtown. You kids go on, and I'll see you later at the house, Tone."

So they left amid the usual roar from Johnny's big convertible.

A few minutes later, after saying good-bye to the boys, Annette made her way on foot down into crowded Main Street.

She was glad Tonia had found something else to do— she might have teased her, because Annette was going to the Malt Shop to see Stan Turner.

As she passed by the Record Shop, she saw a crowd

outside, staring into the window and making excited comments on the display of prizes to be awarded for the different contests. Prominent was a hi-fi stereo record player, an expensive model. A card said that it was the first prize for the singing contest Saturday.

And as close as she could get to the window, her small freckled nose almost against the glass, was Margie Turner.

Annette slipped through the crowd and tapped Margie on the shoulder. "Hi!"

Margie turned around quickly and Annette was astonished to see that she was wearing a long face. "Oh, hi!" Margie answered without much enthusiasm.

"Looking at Stan's prize?" Annette asked gaily. But Margie shook her head soberly. "He isn't going to be in the contest."

"Oh!" Annette was disappointed. "Why, I should think he'd have been the first to enter—the way he can sing!"

Margie shook her head sadly. "He would have, but he can't." She started to turn away, but Annette put her arm around the younger girl's shoulders.

"How about having a soda or something with me at the Malt Shop? I'd like to hear why Stan isn't going to sing."

Margie's eyes brightened at the offer. "A hot fudge sundae?" she asked hopefully.

"Anything you want!" Annette agreed, smiling. And a moment later they were threading their way through crowds of costumed visitors toward the Malt Shop.

"It's the rules," Margie explained as they went. "Everyone who competes has to have a guitar and wear a costume. Stan doesn't have a guitar. And he has no costume. Mom says we're lucky to be eating."

"Well, goodness! I know somebody who has *two* guitars—and I know where I can borrow a real old-time costume! If that's all your brother is worrying about, he can stop right now!"

Margie grabbed her hand. "Let's hurry and tell him!" she cried, pulling Annette through the crowd to the Malt Shop, both of them laughing happily at Annette's simple solution.

"Stan! Hey! Annette's got something to tell you!" Margie climbed a stool and leaned over the counter toward Stan, who was wreathed in steamy vapor and up to his elbows in hot dishwater.

The Malt Shop was crowded. People were finishing and others were pouring in. It was a warm day outside and

promised to be a hectic one for Stan with his combination busboy and dishwasher duties.

"Hi, sis! Hello, Miss McCleod!" He stopped dishwashing to greet them, but as Nick the proprietor passed behind him, he plunged back into the water again to attack the glassware and silver.

It was several minutes before Annette got a chance to talk to him as he dried the silverware. Margie was deep in a large hot fudge sundae, enjoying every mouthful.

"If it's just the guitar that's keeping you from entering the contest," Annette told Stan, "I can borrow one for you. And a costume, too."

"Gosh! You mean it?" Stan's eyes lit up. "I've tried everywhere to borrow a guitar, but no soap!"

"Well, you can quit worrying and go put your name down at contest headquarters," Annette assured him.

"Boy! I sure appreciate it!" He glanced around to see if Nick's back was turned and then leaned over the counter to confide, "They say it'll be on the radio—even in San Francisco! And there'll be some record company people here to listen. If anybody's good enough, it could mean a contract to make records!"

"It's practically yours now!" Annette wasn't fooling.

She felt very happy. And it wasn't all because she was preparing a surprise for Johnny Abbott. "You'll see!"

"About the costume," he asked eagerly, "can you really find one to borrow?" He added frankly, "We can't afford to rent one."

"No need to," she said. "I'll get it from Uncle Genio's collection. He has a luscious caballero outfit, one that used to belong to Governor Pio Pico!"

Stan's face clouded. "Thanks, but I don't want anything from your uncle. Maybe you'd better forget the whole thing." He turned away to gather up a new batch of glasses to wash.

"Stan!" Margie wailed. "Annette's lending it, not Judge Bori!"

"Keep out of it, sis. Time you were going home any-how," he said, avoiding Annette's eyes.

"Wait a minute!" Annette couldn't help being angry. "The guitar isn't my uncle's. And if you had any gump-tion, you'd let your mother fix up a costume for you. I know she can. It's easy. Some colored braid on an old short jacket, and some red and gold ribbons on the guitar! And you can pick out a Mexican song to sing. It'd fit your voice better than rock 'n' roll!"

In spite of himself, Stan listened eagerly and was ashamed of his outburst. "Sorry I flew off the handle again. I'll talk to Mom. And thanks for getting the guitar!"

"'S'all right!" Annette grinned. "I'll get it as soon as I can and bring it to you."

"There she is!" Johnny, with Tonia and two other couples, came surging through the door.

Annette was startled, and surprised to see Johnny waving a copy of the daily *Gazette* as he led the way to her.

"Look! Our little heroine!" Johnny ignored Stan as he spread the paper out on the counter so that Annette could read the headline story about her gallant rescue of her cousin yesterday.

"It has everyone's name in the story!" Tonia told her excitedly.

"Yeah, even us guys that had to drag the two of you out and got our clothes soaked!" Johnny added, with just a tinge of jealousy.

"Say!" Stan leaned over the counter and glanced at the paper. "I want to read that!"

"Then buy a copy!" Johnny said rudely and snatched the paper up. "Come on, Annette! We'll buy you the fanciest sundae this dump fixes up, just to celebrate your publicity!" And in spite of Annette's resistance, he got his arm around her and dragged her to one of the booths that had just been vacated. The others crowded in around them, noisily, and filled up the booth. Johnny took the aisle seat.

"Hey! Get all this mess cleared off this table!" Johnny bellowed to Nick over the hubbub.

"Right away, bud!" Nick called back. He sent Stan over to collect the soiled glasses and silverware.

Annette, crowded unwillingly next to Johnny, tried to catch Stan's eye and give him a friendly smile, but he avoided looking at her and grimly went about his job.

Then, as he picked up the loaded tray and started to leave, he stumbled over something. He tried to keep his balance, failed, and went down, tray and all.

Over the noisy excitement that it caused, Annette heard Johnny say loudly, "What a yokel! Fell over his own feet!" And he laughed loudly.

# 11 *A Change in Plans*

Annette didn't join in the general laughter at Stan's expense as he sprawled in the aisle of the Malt Shop with his glasses and silver scattered about.

She felt almost certain that Johnny Abbott, from his aisle seat in the booth, had swung out his foot and tripped Stan. It was a mean trick and could have hurt Stan.

As it was, there was a small cut on Stan's left forearm from broken glass. He scrambled to his feet and grabbed Johnny by the lapels of his elegant costume. Taken by surprise, Johnny let himself be dragged to his feet by the angry Stan and pulled into the aisle.

"You tripped me, you big ape!" Stan shouted, aiming a doubled fist at Johnny's jaw.

"I never touched you!" Johnny yelled back, ducking the shorter boy's blow and backing off.

Before anything further could happen, Nick hurried over and separated them. "Get that cut fixed up," he told Stan, "and then bring a mop and clean up this floor." And as Stan hesitated, he said, "Go on!"

"Come on, kids," Johnny spoke loudly as Stan turned away, still glowering angrily, and started toward the back room. "Let's get out of this dump and find some place where the local yokels don't trip over their own feet!"

The two young couples, silent and embarrassed, followed Johnny and Tonia out the front door, but Annette lingered to tell Nick angrily, "He *did* trip Stan!"

Nick smiled and nodded. "Thanks, little lady. I was pretty sure he did. I'll put the damage on his father's bill, don't worry!"

Annette felt somewhat relieved as she followed the others outside. At least poor Stan wouldn't have the cost of the broken glasses taken out of his small wages.

"Everybody come on over to the house," Johnny invited. "Pile into the car." He bowed to Annette and waved her into the convertible. "Heroines first!"

But Annette had seen and heard enough of Johnny

Abbott for now. The way he had treated Stan proved to her that her happy plan of borrowing Johnny's old guitar for Stan to play in the singing contest would have no chance of success. Helping Stan would be the last thing Johnny would agree to, even though he seemed positive that he himself had no chance of losing the competition.

"You folks, go on," she told them lightly. "I'll drop by if I get through with my errand."

And Johnny had to be satisfied with that, though he protested that he wanted her to hear his electric guitar and what he could do with it.

She hurried away and lost herself in the crowd. I've got to find some other guitar for Stan, she told herself, after promising so cheerfully!

But neither of the music shops in the small town had a guitar for sale or rent, and when she went back to Deke and Tim to ask their help, they didn't know where she could find either a guitar or anything that looked like one! They were all in use, it seemed.

Tonia came home before her cousin, happy and excited after a fun afternoon of dancing and singing with her friends. And she expected the next morning's paper would carry the news that she had been chosen as queen of the centennial.

"Mom, where's Annette?" she called upstairs, failing to find her cousin in the front parlor or the downstairs playroom. "Isn't she home yet?"

"I haven't seen her." Mrs. Bori leaned over the railing in the upper hallway. "Isn't she with you?"

"No, Mother," Tonia said with a laugh, "or I wouldn't be looking for her!" But for some reason, her mother didn't laugh with her the way she usually did when she'd said something funny.

The door to her father's library opened. "Tonia, will you come in here a moment?" He looked serious.

"Of course, Dad!" She went in and he closed the door. The judge came to the point at once. "Honey, there's something I have to tell you. Last night, the committee picked you to be queen—"

"Oh, Dad! That's super! Have they sent word to the *Gazette*? Will there be a special edition out tonight?"

He shook his head slowly. "They're waiting. You see, dear, when Annette saved you from drowning yesterday, it seemed to me that it was only fair to suggest to the committee that she be chosen queen for her bravery."

"Oh!" Tonia's eyes were wide with surprise. Tears

welled up in them as she stared at her father. "D-did they?" she whispered.

"Not yet. The vote last night was official, and even though Joe Patton and several others agreed that it would be a fine gesture, they all thought it should be up to you yourself, and no one else. You can be queen, or you can call Joe Patton at his office and tell him you want Annette to have the honor."

"I won't give it up! I've been counting on it for days! I've made all my arrangements!" Tonia burst into violent sobs and ran out of the room and upstairs.

Her mother was waiting in the upper hallway and tried to stop her and put her arms around the crying girl, but Tonia pushed her aside and ran into her own room.

A moment later, Mrs. Bori heard the key turn in the lock, and when she tiptoed over to listen anxiously at the door, she heard Tonia's muffled sobs.

The judge was coming heavily up the stairs. He didn't need to ask his wife where Tonia was. He could hear the sobs himself.

"I knew what would happen! My poor baby!" She was on the verge of tears herself.

Judge Bori knew what he would be in for in the next

few minutes if he lingered; he turned around and went downstairs considerably faster than he had come up, and took refuge in the quiet of his library.

When Annette finally climbed the hill, warm and tired, and came into the big house, she was surprised at the complete silence she found. There was no sign of any of the family, except that she could hear the judge pacing the floor of his study.

In the kitchen, Katey was getting dinner in gloomy silence, though usually she was ready to talk a blue streak at every chance.

"Has there been some bad news, Katey?" Annette asked anxiously.

But Katey just grunted loudly and snapped, "Nobody's told the help, Miss Annette. But there's been a spot of cryin' goin' on upstairs, and the judge has been talkin' to himself like mad in his library!"

Annette ran upstairs and knocked on her cousin's door. At first, Tonia didn't answer. Then she called out faintly that she had a headache and was lying down. So Annette went away, puzzled, to her own room to freshen up for dinner.

Tonia sat up, with a last sniff, and eyed the damp pillow

she had been crying into. Even across the room, she could see in her dresser mirror that her eyes were red and swollen. She looked like anything but a queen!

For a long time, she sat thinking. Then she rose suddenly, went over to the dresser, and powdered her face carefully till almost all trace of tears was hidden. She even managed to smile at herself as she fluffed out her ponytail.

Judge Bori, trying unhappily to concentrate on the latest volume of California Law and Procedure, heard his library door open a couple minutes later.

"Hi, Dad!" Tonia was smiling a little uncertainly as she came in. "May I use your phone? I want to call Mr. Patton and tell him I think it's a wonderful idea for Annette to be queen."

For a moment, the judge stared, only half believing he was hearing right. Then, "You bet you can, dear! Help yourself!" And as he sat beaming proudly at his daughter, she put in the call and gave her message to the chairman of the committee in a firm voice that she even managed to make sound cheerful and happy.

And actually, she wasn't too unhappy. Tonia was like her father. It might take her a little while to adjust herself,

but once it was done, she didn't brood over it. There were a couple of angles that still disturbed her, but she felt sure they could be taken care of easily.

They broke the news to Annette at the dinner table.

She was amazed. "But why?" Annette asked them.

And when Tonia told her why they thought she deserved the honor, Annette smiled and shook her head. "You're darlings, all of you. But Tonia's the queen, and that's that! Besides, I've promised to ride on Deke and Tim's float."

"I'm afraid you'll have to break that promise, dear," Judge Bori told her. "The story has been given to the *Gazette* by now, and the special edition is probably on the presses at this moment."

And Annette had to let it go at that.

But later on, in Tonia's room, the two girls talked it over as they put on the pretty gowns they were to wear Saturday night at the dance.

A newspaper reporter and a photographer were due at any minute to interview both of them and take their pictures for the "Souvenir Edition" that was coming out Saturday morning.

"I can't help feeling guilty," Annette admitted. "I know

everyone's been counting on your being queen. And I don't want them thinking I snatched it from you somehow."

"Nobody's going to think anything so silly!" Tonia insisted.

Annette frowned. "I bet Johnny Abbott will! I heard him tell Lola that he'd be riding with you in the parade!"

"I *did* promise," Tonia admitted, looking wistful. "Now he'll be with you—" She hesitated, then added, with a question in her voice, "I suppose?"

Annette looked at her sharply. "Do you want him to?"

"I don't care." Tonia tossed her head, but Annette wasn't fooled.

"Well, *I* do. And I'm going to ask Stan Turner instead!"

Tonia looked shocked. "You can't ask *him*! Everybody knows his father's in prison for—for a terrible crime!"

"What does that have do with it? It wasn't Stan who did it! He's a very nice person."

Tonia shook her head. "The committee would be awfully angry. It would cause all sorts of talk. Everyone knows Dad sentenced his father. You just can't do it, 'Nette!"

Annette looked unhappy. "Okay. I guess maybe you're right." And she added after a moment, "So I'll ride all alone and like it!"

Tonia smiled. Annette could see she was greatly relieved. Then suddenly, Tonia looked worried again.

"Now what?" She put her arm around Tonia.

"I was thinking—maybe you'd better let Johnny ride with you anyhow—because you'll have to invite him to be Prince Charming at the square dance on Saturday night after he wins the singing contest!"

"Huh!" Annette grinned impishly. "He hasn't won it yet!"

Tonia looked curious. "Sounds like you don't think he will."

Annette laughed and squeezed her tall blond cousin. "Could be!" she admitted.

The lights of a car flashed through the second-story window onto the bedroom ceiling.

"Uh-oh! Somebody's coming up the hill! We'd better finish dressing. It's probably the men from the *Gazette!*" Tonia reminded Annette hastily, and they both started rushing around, making the final adjustments in their costumes.

It was the reporter and photographer, as Tonia had guessed. But there was a second car following them. It was a large, expensive convertible, and Johnny was at the wheel.

He was in his gambler costume and had his guitar.

He'd been on his way home to do some practicing for the contest when he'd seen the reporter's car turn up the hill and recognized the two men in it. He had promptly followed. If there were pictures being taken, he might be able to get into them. He knew Tonia would be agreeable to it. She'd probably tell them he was going to ride on her queen float tomorrow, and they'd be glad to include him in a shot or two.

The *Gazette* men were carrying the camera up the steep steps as Johnny parked behind their car. It was old-fashioned equipment, and heavy.

"Need any help, Jerry?" Johnny asked, running up the steps after them.

"Nope!" The reporter was a local boy.

"Be glad to give you a hand!" he persisted amiably. "Tonia'll want me in some of the shots. I'll be riding on the queen's float with her tomorrow."

"Tonia? It's Annette McCleod who's going to be on the float." The reporter pressed the doorbell button. "Wise up, bud. You're off the beam."

Katey came to the door. "Oh, it's you, Jerry Finn. Wipe your feet an' come in."

The two *Gazette* men obediently did as they were told. They knew better than to disobey when Katey commanded.

But Johnny Abbott stayed outside. He hid back in the shadows as Katey admitted the others, and he remained there as Katey closed the door without noticing him.

He was practically in a state of shock. Annette the queen instead of Tonia! He wondered how it had happened. Not that it mattered *how*. The cold fact was that he was not going to ride on the queen's float the next day — after telling his friends that he would!

He had no illusions about the way Annette felt toward him. She had shown it several times.

He didn't have a chance. And half the town would be laughing at him after the parade . . . unless . . . unless he could persuade Tonia to use her influence on Annette to get him the invitation!

He got back in his car, smiling. He felt sure he could talk Tonia into it. She was pretty gaga over him, he told himself. It should be easy.

# *12*  *The Guitar*

There were many people in Lost Creek who didn't sleep that night. Half the town was getting ready for the next afternoon's "Stupendous Parade of the Pioneers and Three—Count 'Em—*Three* Bands!"

Then there were others, like the Turners in the tiny house outside of town, whose busy fingers and hopeful hearts were set on the Big Event of the day after that: the song contest that could mean so much more to its winner than just an expensive prize. Winning could mean a whole career for some young singer.

Mrs. Turner had taken one of her husband's old suits, the coat of which could be shortened and trimmed with tinsel and bright ribbons to look like a Mexican jacket.

And she and Margie pinned, pasted, and sewed till nearly dawn. The tight caballero pants were easier to render, with a tuck here, a slit up the sides of the legs, and more bright ribbon sewed on the seams.

By daylight, Stan had a costume of sorts. He would qualify for the contest now.

Or would he? Where was the guitar he must have?

"Don't worry, Mother!" He stood straight and tall in his bright outfit. "Annette says she knows where to get it. She'll have it for me this morning, I'm sure."

"But it's a long time since you played," Mrs. Turner worried. "Do you remember the chords?"

"I'll practice all night till I do!" he assured her gravely. "But it shouldn't be too much of a job. I've picked out a number without too many changes."

"Do you think you ought to phone her this morning?" Mrs. Turner asked anxiously.

"Gosh! I can't do that! It'd look as if I didn't believe she was telling me the truth. I *know* she can get it."

But a few hours later, when Stan had left for the Malt Shop and Mrs. Turner was getting ready to go to work at the Lunchroom, she decided that it would do no harm if *she* were to phone Annette about it. In the excitement of the celebration, Annette might have forgotten her promise. "I'll call her from the Lunchroom, first chance I get," she resolved. "I'm sure she won't mind."

Johnny Abbott was another who hadn't slept much that night. He had tossed and turned and fumed and fussed over his situation. Although he told himself repeatedly during the dark hours that he'd have no difficulty persuading Tonia to speak to Annette about letting him ride with her on the queen's float, he wasn't sure of it.

So morning found him mounting the Bori front steps with a handsome bouquet of native golden leopard lilies for each girl.

The *Gazette* had already been delivered, with most of its front page devoted to the story of Tonia's handing over the crown of queen to her brave cousin Annette.

"Hey, chicks!" He strode in, looking very handsome in his costume. "Let me be the first to greet the new queen!" He bowed to Annette and handed her one of the bouquets.

"The phone's been ringing all morning," Tonia said, a slight tinkle of ice in her voice. "You're about the twentieth!"

Johnny laughed and held out the second bunch of lilies to Tonia. "For you, for being the best sport in the state of California! And the prettiest blonde!"

"Goodness! You even talk like a gambler in the movies!" Tonia giggled and buried her face in the lilies. He was already forgiven.

Johnny beamed, but Annette thought, Oh, brother!

"Telephone for Annette!" Aunt Betta called, and Annette hurried to answer it. Half the people who had called were strangers to her, but she had done her best all morning to let them know that she was happy to have their congratulations.

But it was a different sort of call this time. It was Mrs. Turner on the line. And Annette was genuinely glad to hear from her.

The older woman told her frankly, "I know how busy you must be, my dear, but I wondered if you still think you can get that guitar you mentioned, for Stan."

"I'll get it this morning and run right over to the Malt Shop with it," Annette told her cheerfully. But when they had hung up, she wasn't so sure. She went back to Johnny and Tonia, wondering how she could borrow the guitar without mentioning Stan's name. It was a ticklish situation.

In the few minutes that she had been gone, Johnny had seized the chance to ask Tonia the favor he had really come for. And Tonia had promptly told him, "Annette isn't going to ask *anyone* to ride on her float with her. So there's no use of my asking her!"

"Look," he argued desperately, "you don't have to be jealous. Annette doesn't mean a thing to me. But I've told everybody I'm going to ride on that float. I'll look like a dope if I don't. Be a good sport! Tell her you promised me. You did!"

"Sorry!" Tonia said coldly. "Do your own begging. It won't do you any good anyhow. You're the last one she'd have!"

Annette came bouncing in at that moment. She could see in a flash that there had been a storm, but she hoped it was just another momentary upset.

"Annette!" Johnny flashed a defiant look at Tonia as he spoke to her cousin. "What are my chances to ride on the float with you this afternoon?"

Tonia waited, wearing a smug little smile. Annette would tell him no without any frills!

But Annette didn't. She hesitated, then smiled at Johnny. "I planned to ride alone. But I'll make a deal with you."

Tonia gasped, but Johnny agreed excitedly. "Anything you say!"

"Okay, then. Lend me your old guitar, and I'll let you ride on my float this afternoon in the parade!"

"It's a deal! I'll dash home and get it for you right now!" And a moment later, the front door slammed after him and they heard the roar of his motor.

"Oh, Annette!" Tonia wailed, bursting into tears. "You promised! You said you wouldn't have him! And now look!"

Annette slipped an arm around her cousin's shoulders. "Listen, silly! Johnny's a big bag of wind, and you can keep him, believe me! I knew he wouldn't lend me his guitar without asking a lot of questions. And I've simply *got* to have it! So—I had to make a deal!"

"Who's the guitar for?" Tonia felt pretty sure she knew, but she had to ask.

"You won't tell Johnny?"

"Cross my heart!"

"It's for Stan Turner! He has no way of getting one, and he can't be in the contest without it."

"Stan Turner!" Tonia sniffed disdainfully.

"You know how he and Johnny feel about each other! Johnny would never do anything to help him. You won't tell?"

"I already promised, didn't I? Besides, I hope Stan wins

the contest with that guitar. It would serve Johnny right!"

Within a remarkably short space of time, Johnny was back with his old guitar in its leather case.

"Thanks, Johnny!" Annette took it, smiling sweetly and blinking her long dark eyelashes at him. "You're a livin' doll!"

"What do you want it for?" Johnny asked curiously. "I didn't know you could play!"

"Lots of things you don't know!" Annette laughed and winked at Tonia who was watching them both soberly. Tonia still wasn't sure she liked the situation.

Annette hurried toward the door with the guitar. She paused in the doorway to smile back at Johnny. "See you around two fifteen at the parade assembly lot!"

"Okay, chickie! I'll be there!" Johnny called after her before she closed the door.

Annette went to the phone and a few moments later she had Stan Turner on the wire. "Hold everything! I'm on my way over—with *it*!" she told him merrily.

Then she ran out the back door to get the Monster from the garage and go downtown.

Back inside the house, Johnny tried to put his arm around Tonia's waist. He was feeling on top of the world.

But Tonia drew away, pouting. "Don't!" she said crossly.

"Say, what *are* you two girls plotting?" he asked. "I bet you want to get rid of me so you two can work up a surprise musical act for tomorrow night! Is that it?"

"Why don't you ask *her*?" Tonia tossed her blond head. "You might get a shock!"

"What's that supposed to mean?" he scowled.

"That's for you to find out," she answered sweetly. "I hear her motor starting up out there! You can catch her if you hurry!"

"Maybe I'll do just that!" Johnny barked. And slamming on his expensive, wide-brimmed black hat, he stalked out, slamming the door behind him.

Tonia stood a moment and then burst into tears again. "I hate you, Johnny Abbott!" she wailed and ran up to her room. Another door slammed.

Annette backed the Monster out of the garage. It was the first time she had taken the white sports car out since her arrival. "We'll go by the Malt Shop and then I'll take you for some air. You've been a good little Monster, waiting so patiently." And she turned its nose toward the circular driveway in front of the house.

But she had to pull her emergency brake on quickly as

Johnny ran down from the porch and planted himself in the middle of the drive.

"What's the idea? You trying to collect some insurance?" Annette was a little shaken, and angry.

"What's the idea, yourself?" Johnny barked at her. "Where are you going so fast with my guitar? What's Tonia mean by saying I might get a shock if I found out what you're doing with it?"

Annette glared at him a moment, then she sighed. There was no use trying to sidestep again. She might as well come out with the truth. "I'm lending it to a friend for the contest tomorrow. That's all."

"Who?" He scowled suspiciously.

"Stan Turner," she told him quietly. "Stan needs a guitar, and there isn't one in town he can rent or borrow."

Johnny strode to the side of the car, reached in, and plucked his guitar case from the seat beside Annette. "Well, he's not getting mine, the moocher!"

"We made a deal, if you remember," Annette reminded him coldly. "You can't weasel out of it now."

"Oh, can't I?" Johnny's face was red with anger. And without another word, he stalked off to his own car, threw the guitar into the back, and flopped into the driver's seat.

A moment later, the engine roared deafeningly, and with a squeal of tires, the heavy coupe took off down the hill at a decidedly illegal rate of speed.

Annette sat slumped behind her wheel, disgusted. The worst part of it was that now Stan wouldn't be able to take part in the contest. And the poor guy was waiting, right now, for that guitar.

Now she'd have to break the news to him that she had no guitar. It wasn't going to be easy. But there was no use stalling. She might as well get it over with.

She started her motor again and drove slowly down the hill, feeling miserable.

When she reached Main Street, she noticed a crowd milling around the corner by the old fire station. Must have been an accident, Annette thought soberly.

She drove carefully to avoid the curious crowd, but as she passed the corner, she stole a quick look toward the center of the disturbance.

She was so surprised that she almost killed her engine. Johnny Abbott's big convertible had crashed into the old wooden sidewalk in front of the fire station, and Johnny, angrily protesting, was being escorted by a stern-looking policeman toward the police station next door.

Tagging right along, and shouting angry accusations at Johnny, was a member of the Queen Committee, an elderly and important citizen. He was waving his cane threateningly at Johnny as they disappeared into the police station.

Annette hurriedly parked in the first vacant spot she could find on the narrow side street and rushed back to find out what had happened. She had a feeling that by making him angry, she was partly to blame for Johnny's predicament.

The crowd was beginning to scatter, still discussing the elderly citizen's narrow escape from being hit by "that big guy in the convertible."

The fire chief was out in front of his station, eying the car parked on the sidewalk, blocking the fire engine. "Somebody'll have to move this heap, or we'll tow it away and lock it up!" he told the indifferent crowd.

"I'll do it. I'm a friend of Johnny Abbott's," Annette told him.

"That's fine, Miss McCleod. I hope the goon appreciates it. He'd be paying a double fine if it stood here much longer."

The keys were still in the ignition, and Annette had no

problem backing the big car off the sidewalk and into a parking space up the street that was just being vacated.

As she stepped out of the convertible, she glanced into the back. The guitar case had been jolted off the rear seat onto the floor and was lying there temptingly.

Annette hesitated a moment. Then she reached in and took it. She found a small piece of paper in her purse and scribbled on it: "I took the guitar back. Please, don't be angry. I'll look for you at the float. Your friend, Annette."

"There!" she told herself. "That ought to smooth his feathers!" Then she laid the slip of paper on the driver's seat where he couldn't miss seeing it.

She was starting away with the guitar when she suddenly realized that she was carrying off Johnny's car keys.

She went back to the car and opened the door. But before she slipped into the seat, she cast a quick look toward the people passing by on the sidewalk. Nobody seemed to be looking toward the car. It should be safe to hide the keys under the floor mat. She remembered Johnny saying it was his favorite spot to leave them, though personally she never took chances like that herself. Uncle Archie had warned her that it was one of the first places that a car thief would look.

But this was a little town, and everyone seemed too busy having a good time to think about stealing cars.

So she bent over and quickly slipped the keys under the floor mat, sat a couple of minutes more, to be sure she didn't appear to be rushing away carelessly, and then got out with the guitar case. Just to be sure, she glanced at the sidewalk crowds again as they jostled and pushed past, everyone having a splendid time in costume. No one seemed to be the least bit interested in her actions.

She went down the street with the guitar case, toward the Malt Shop.

She had scarcely lost herself in the crowd when a roughly dressed, black-bearded man sauntered slowly out of a doorway across the street—and toward the car.

He was a hungry-looking man, with desperation in his deeply sunken eyes. And for the past couple of hours he had lingered in that doorway, trying to work out a problem of survival. Just by chance he had noticed the pretty young girl in the big car. He had watched her idly at first, and then with keen interest. When she had gone away, at last, a hard smile had twisted his mouth.

He had found the answer to his problem.

# 13 *Annette's Secret*

The Malt Shop was doing a brisk business, although it was well before lunchtime. When Annette came in with the guitar in its case, she had to thread her way through a cheerful, laughing mob of out-of-town customers. Most of them were intent on buying catchpenny souvenirs of the celebration, but all the stools at the counter were filled, and Stan was rushing about helping to serve.

It was several minutes before Annette had a chance to speak to him and give him the guitar.

"Wow!" Stan grinned. "You really did it!"

"Told you I would!" Annette said with a laugh. "Now don't you dare lose that contest!"

Stan sobered. "Gosh, I don't know if I'm that good. If

I do win, it'll be luck," he admitted earnestly, "but I'll do my darnedest!"

"I know you will," Annette told him confidently, getting serious herself.

Nick was bellowing for his busboy to come clear a table, so Annette said a hasty good-bye and ran off.

As she passed the spot where she had parked Johnny Abbott's convertible, she noticed that it was gone. He must have finished his business at the police station and left, thought Annette. She hoped he'd had a good lecturing.

By now, she thought uneasily, he was probably stewing over that note she had left him. She expected to find him, or a message from him, at the Bori home when she arrived. I only hope he won't go tearing into the Malt Shop and grab that guitar back from Stan, she thought. Maybe I shouldn't have taken it.

But it was too late to think about that now.

Instead of going for a ride, as she had planned, she turned the Monster back up the hill to the big house. Might as well face the hullabaloo Johnny was sure to raise!

But there was no word from Johnny awaiting her. And as the lunch hour passed and the time for assembling the parade came closer, Annette decided that Johnny had probably decided not to make an issue over the guitar again, at least not till after he had ridden in the parade at her side and had all the publicity he seemed to crave.

After that, he would probably insist on taking back the guitar, in spite of their "deal," unless she could talk him out of it during the parade. She'd try hard.

Maybe, if she could persuade Tonia to ride with her, too, as a "Royal Princess" or something like that, the two of them could shame Johnny into not going back on his deal about the guitar. She planned to talk to Tonia about it directly after lunch.

But Tonia had made other arrangements for the parade. She was bubbling over with them. Judge Bori had cooked up a happy surprise for his daughter because she had been so bighearted about resigning her queenship.

Old Mike, the handyman, drove in from the garage in the handsome old carriage that was one of the main attractions of the judge's private museum. He had polished the brass-mounted lamps and wiped the dust from the leather upholstery. The body was shining like new. To top it all off, the judge had hired a pair of high-stepping grays to draw the carriage in the parade.

It was an open carriage, and Judge and Mrs. Bori would share it with Tonia, with Mike on the box.

The two girls dressed in a flurry of excitement and many giggles. Several times, Annette almost told her cousin about the guitar, but each time she decided not to, mostly because she didn't want Tonia to blame herself because Johnny had snatched it away from her after Tonia had hinted about what Annette was going to do with it.

There were half a dozen calls for Tonia from her friends, all wanting to know what she was going to do in the parade and begging her to join them. But she was sweetly mysterious and told them all, "Just look for me. I'll be there!"

But there was no call from Johnny for either of them. Annette decided that she had been right, that Johnny would wait till after he'd ridden in the parade before quarreling with her and getting the guitar back.

Annette was framing speeches that she might use to persuade Johnny to let Stan have the guitar for the contest, but none of them seemed likely to succeed.

Then Johnny failed to show up at the parade assembly grounds, and the parade started with a puzzled queen riding alone on her float.

* * *

Annette could not know that Johnny was still locked up—and would stay there till his father bailed him out. Mr. Abbott was away fishing at his favorite spot in the High Sierras.

Police Chief Trujillo was a good friend of Johnny's father. As a matter of fact, he had been invited on that fishing trip. But he had given it up to remain on duty during the celebration. This didn't add to his good humor or incline him to be lenient with his old friend's spoiled brat of a son—especially when Johnny talked back impudently after speeding and endangering the life of one of Lost Creek's leading citizens, Jedediah Joralemon, the old gent with the cane.

Consequently, Police Chief Trujillo had no compunction about locking up Johnny Abbott. It would teach him not to take the laws so lightly, and to keep a civil tongue in his blond head.

However, Chief Trujillo made one exception. He sent one of his men up to the fishing camp—in a rattletrap pickup truck that couldn't make over fifteen miles an hour—to inform Abbott senior that his son was at odds with the law. He should be back with Mr. Abbott, or bail money, by evening, thought Chief Trujillo. And probably with some succulent trout, to boot!

The sound of the parade wafted into Johnny's temporary home and made him angrier than before, if that were possible. Band music, to the accompaniment of loud applause, meant the parade had started. And he wasn't in it.

It was a fine parade! Everybody said so, loudly and with deep conviction. First, the Union High School band came stepping out proudly behind its drum major. And the line of pom-pom girls was as well drilled as any city outfit, the tourists declared. There was even a baton twirler, a cute youngster who only dropped her baton twice during the up- and downhill course of Main Street.

Deke and Tim's float came next. Deke, fake whiskers blowing in the Sierra breeze, knelt beside his aluminum-foil creek and panned solemnly for gold, while Tim tended a fake fire and cooked a pot of beans in front of the one-walled cabin. The crowd gave them lots of applause, especially when a spotted dog ran in front of the float, and Benny Barton from the Auto Hire brought the float to a sudden stop that sent Deke headfirst into his fake creek and toppled half the cabin wall onto the cook.

But by the time they passed the reviewing stand in front of the Record Shop, they had recovered. And the judges gave them a good hand as they moved past.

A group of girls and boys in pioneer costumes rode on a loaded hay wagon, singing "Clementine" more or less in harmony and playing ukuleles and banjos.

An ancient locomotive went by, mounted on the back of a truck and decorated with bunting and signs that proclaimed it as the first to have made the weekly run between Goldlight and Lost Creek on the narrow gauge railroad—now, alas, gone forever.

Then came the second band, the combined Odd Fellows and Elks, making a joyful noise and heralding the advent of Queen Annette perched on her gilded throne.

Annette smiled and waved the whole length of the parade and called, "Hello, there!" right and left, as the crowds cheered. But there was so much excitement that even though she tried to recognize faces as she passed, she could only make out a blur of smiles and waving arms.

It was only as she was carried past the Malt Shop that she caught a glimpse of a familiar face. It was Stan, standing on a folding chair in the doorway, waving to her over the heads of the crowd.

But nowhere did she see any sign of Johnny. And it puzzled her a great deal.

Judge Bori and his wife and Tonia, in their elegant turnout, gathered as much applause as the queen. The crowd had a warm spot in its heart for the pretty blond girl who had stepped aside so they could honor her brave young cousin. They were eager to let her know it, and Tonia was frankly delighted with their cheers.

The third band, small in number but filled with enthusiasm, played loudly just behind Judge Bori's carriage. And behind them came a float depicting the famous Morgan Hill Mine in its palmy days. The Chamber of Commerce had spent weeks on it, copying old prints. And it was as complete as they could make it, down to its miniature miners.

Then came a motley collection of ore wagons, freight wagons, buggies loaded with pretty girls, and bearded "miners" with burros and prospecting equipment.

Small boys of all ages brought up the rear and, as always, had more fun than anybody else, trying to keep in step. And so the parade ended and everyone went home.

It was after dark before the pickup truck came back from the fishing camp with a note and a check from

Johnny Abbott's father. There was also a basket filled with plump trout for the chief of police.

A few minutes later, Johnny found himself free on bail. After a short but stern lecture, he went to look for his car at the fire station where he had left it parked on the side-walk. "Somebody moved it. I dunno who it was. Chief didn't say. Just said somebody drove it off somewheres to get it out of our way." The night man was not particularly concerned or even interested.

But Johnny couldn't find it on the length of Main Street or up the side streets. Somebody had moved it, all right—moved it clear out of sight!

He stormed back to the police station, but he got little sympathy from the chief. "Should've known better than to leave your keys in it. Tch! Tch!"

"What are you going to do about getting it back?" Johnny demanded angrily, ignoring his own guilt.

"Well, now, guess I'll send out a bulletin. Figure who-ever took it will abandon it when it runs out o' gas. Big car like that costs too much to run."

"Thanks for nothing!" Johnny turned and stalked out.

"Bulletin can wait," the chief told himself. "Walking for a few days might teach that young whippersnapper a lesson he needs!" And he left for home with the basket full of tasty trout and the knowledge that his old friend John Abbott, Sr., would agree wholeheartedly with the policy he had adopted.

They had held many a discussion over Johnny, and the chief knew that Johnny was just undisciplined, not mean.

Johnny started walking home. It was only a few blocks from the center of town to the Abbott summer place, but Johnny was like a great many of his generation—he never walked when he could ride. Maybe I'll drop in on Annette and borrow her car for a couple of days, he thought. But he changed his mind before he was halfway up the hill to the Bori home. He had a very strong hunch that Annette would be unsympathetic after the way he had snatched back the guitar. And Tonia and he had parted company rather angrily that morning. He might not be welcome just then.

So Johnny went on home and gloomily practiced "The Roving Gambler" on his guitar till well past midnight. He was rather pleased with his own performance and went to sleep a little later, firmly convinced that he had every chance of winning the contest.

And when he *did* win it, he decided, Queen Annette

would have no excuse to ignore his claims. She'd have to choose him as her Prince Charming to lead the grand march with her the following night. If she hesitated, he'd appeal to the committee. He'd explain that it had all been arranged with Tonia. And when she abdicated as queen, Annette was bound to keep Tonia's promises. He felt sure they'd agree.

But Johnny wasn't the only one who was up late, working on his contest song. Stan Turner was still going over and over the old ballad that he planned to sing at competition. It was one that his mother had remembered from her own childhood, sung to her by *her* grandmother:

"Swift roved the Indian maid, bright Alfarata,
Where swept the waters of the Blue Juniata."

Mrs. Turner had sent Margie sleepily to bed, but she herself was still adding improvements to Stan's costume.

"It looks pretty bright, doesn't it?" Stan asked doubtfully. Then he added hastily, "I sure like it, Mom!"

"I'm so happy you do, dear." She sighed wearily. "It'll look fine in the pictures they take when you get first prize!"

"*If* I do!" Stan corrected her quickly.

"You will," she answered in a firm voice, "if there's such a thing as fairness in the judging."

And in her room at the Bori home, Annette was awake till nearly dawn. The thing that was troubling her was why Johnny hadn't come to ride on the parade float after he had found her note in the car—and whether he had stormed over to the Malt Shop and made a scene getting his guitar back from Stan, an innocent party in the whole deal!

She wished that she hadn't tried to help. Maybe she had made things worse for Stan.

Well, she would find out in the morning.

# 14 *Disaster!*

Along toward morning, the distant rumble of thunder sounded through the Sierra foothills and lightning flashed in the high mountains. But the storm passed over Lost Creek with only a few sprinkles that washed the dust off the roadside bushes and left the leaves of the tall oaks and ailanthus trees sparklingly clean.

There were sighs of relief when the sun rose, warm and unclouded, on one of Lost Creek's biggest days. The singing competition had been advertised far and wide. There was a "remote broadcast" arranged by a Sacramento television station, and at least two national radio networks had sent men to cover the event. It would be the biggest boost the old mining town had ever received and would mean money in everyone's pocket all summer and fall.

Rain would have been disastrous, but a kindly providence had sent the storm circling around Lost Creek.

At the Bori home, no one slept after six o'clock that morning. There was too much excitement in the air.

By the time Katey came to the foot of the staircase and tinkled the old silver bell that meant breakfast was almost ready, both girls were dressed in the starched white dresses that they were to wear at the singing contest right after lunch.

They came down the stairs arm in arm, making such a pretty picture in their costumes that Judge Bori, coming in from the porch with his morning paper, stood and looked at them and shook his head sadly.

"Goodness, Dad! What's wrong? Don't you like our dresses?" Tonia asked disappointedly.

"Indeed, I do!" He had a twinkle in his eye. "I was just feeling sad to think how styles have changed since pretty girls were pretty girls and were happy just being that!"

"Hmmph!" Aunt Betta replied from the dining room. "I'm sure my grandmother could beat my grandfather at tennis, Genio Bori. Even in skirts like that!"

And everyone had a good laugh at the judge, who threw up his hands and admitted defeat.

All through breakfast, Annette kept listening for the phone to ring and Katey to call, "For you, Miss Annette." She expected to hear at any moment from Stan, to say that Johnny had taken back the guitar and now Stan couldn't sing in the contest.

She had no way of knowing that Johnny not only hadn't found her note in the car but hadn't even found the car!

Tonia listened for the phone, too. She was ready to forgive Johnny for rushing away angrily the day before when she had teased him about what Annette was going to do with the borrowed guitar. She hadn't heard from him since, and neither had any of the kids, Tim or Deke or Lola. She hoped he'd phone before the contest started, so she could wish him good luck. But Johnny didn't telephone.

Johnny was quite busy, getting a lecture from his father. Mr. Abbott had sacrificed several days of his fishing trip to get home and give his son a choice of driving carefully from then on, or giving up his car for the rest of school vacation.

When the elder Abbott discovered that Johnny's car had been stolen, with the keys in it, he really let go.

"That does it!" He fumed. "If that car isn't found, you'll do without one!"

And Mr. Abbott stamped out to his own expensive car and drove into town to see his old friend Police Chief Trujillo.

"Got the description of the car onto the wires, first thing this morning," Trujillo told him, as they drank coffee together in the police station. "No answers yet. But give 'em time. Big car like that's a white elephant unless a man's pockets are lined with silver."

"Well, there's no hurry," John Abbott assured him. "It's well insured against anything. Had to be, with Johnny driving. Good boy, but bad temper. Makes a poor driver."

"Right!" Trujillo nodded, pouring another cup of coffee. "Walkin' makes good exercise," he added. Then, with a wink, " 'Specially for the young!" He hadn't walked more than half a block himself in years, and he knew that Abbott hadn't either—unless it was to wade in a trout stream.

The stands at the county fairground filled up early for the contest. There was a royal box at one side of the platform on which the contestants were to appear, and it had a canopy of bunting over it, for the queen's comfort, and half a dozen chairs from Gray's undertaking parlor.

The platform was shaded, too, and well wired by both the radio stations and the remote-control unit from the capital. Big spotlights stood at either side, to be used while the television cameras were rolling.

The contest committee members, with solemn faces befitting their importance, were seated in the front row of the audience, and a few minutes later, Queen Annette and her party arrived and entered the royal box.

Annette, pink-cheeked and excited, was a picture in her white dress, carrying an armful of fairylike mariposa lilies from the fields outside of town. Tonia and Lola followed, holding wild lavender peas from the hedges along the roadside. Those lilies and peas were perennial symbols of the Mother Lode country, and the crowd gave all three girls hearty applause as they recognized them. No fragile hothouse roses for these pioneers!

The contestants were assembling under the trees behind the platform. They would be called up, one by one. And the Elks band, in uniform, would play selections after each performance to give the judges a chance to discuss what they had just heard.

Carl Bradley, of Astral Records, had driven down from the city to hear the contestants. It was his job as a new talent scout. He had little hope of discovering any startling talents. He had attended too many of these local celebrations. But there was always a faint hope—and the possibility that if he didn't "cover" the event, a scout from some other company might, and find a star! He had purposely kept from identifying himself to any of the judges or contestants. Too many tried to put pressure on when they found out he was a talent scout. It could be very annoying.

So Bradley took his place in the audience of tourists and locals and prepared himself for an afternoon of boredom.

The first three contestants lived up to his pessimistic expectations. A boy in cowboy costume, plunking his guitar awkwardly, sang "Home on the Range" slightly off-key.

Then Tim came on as a tramp and did "The Big Rock Candy Mountains" without much inspiration. He got a black mark in the talent scout's book when he forgot the lyrics.

Deke was better, as he did some fancy old-fashioned clog dancing and guitar twirling to go with his rendering of "Sweet Alice Ben Bolt." But he got so breathless from the dancing that nobody could hear his singing. So the effect on the talent scout was nothing, though the audience loved it.

Then it was Stan Turner's time to perform. There was a
buzz of comment among the townspeople as he came onto
the platform. They were remembering his father.

Annette felt a load lift off her mind as she saw him
stride out, guitar in hand, his Mexican costume glittering
in the sun. Johnny hadn't snatched back the guitar, after
all!

"Why, he looks almost handsome!" Tonia whispered in
surprise.

Annette just smiled and leaned back in her chair. He'd
surprise a lot of people today, she felt sure, once he began
to sing!

A few soft chords, and then began the ballad of the
Indian girl Alfarata and her warrior lover, on the banks of
the Blue Juniata.

It was an old familiar song to the Mother Lode. They
had heard it in their cradles, sung softly as Stan was doing
it. And when he had finished, there was a louder round of
applause than any heard so far that day. But it all came
from the older folks.

Then, as the applause died away, Stan grinned and
struck a couple of lively chords as he swung into a rhythmic version of the same old song. After the first surprised

reaction, the young ones in the audience were tapping their feet and nodding their heads. Soon, as the rhythm caught them, they began clapping in time to the beat.

Carl Bradley of Astral Records sat up straight as Stan swung through the song to a smashing climax and the kids clapped, swayed, and squealed along with him.

Behind the platform, waiting to go on next, Johnny heard it all and scowled uneasily. He could see the television men hard at work capturing the enthusiastic reaction to Stan Turner, live, for the city viewers. For the first time, he felt sorry that he had insisted on being the last contestant. Stan was going to be hard to follow, electric guitar or no electric guitar.

The stage manager beckoned him up on the stage to stand ready to come on when Stan finished. Johnny went reluctantly, mounting the steps slowly.

Stan was starting the chorus again, after yells from the kids of "More! More!"

"What's the hurry? What about the band number?" Johnny demanded.

"We have to cut it. Running too long. You're on next."

"Hold on a minute! You oughta give 'em time to cool down!"

"You don't have to go on at all, buddy. It's no skin off my nose if you don't!" He was a local boy.

"Oh, yeah?" Johnny snarled. Then, suddenly, he gave a snort of surprise. He had just spotted an empty guitar case lying open right at his feet, behind the scenery flat. "Hey, that's my missing guitar case! How did it get there?"

"Belongs to Stan Turner. He brought his guitar in it!"

"*My* guitar, you mean! The dirty little thief!" Johnny was shouting now. "So that's what became of my guitar! I might have known he'd be the one that stole it!" He started out onto the stage, where Stan was just finishing the last notes of the swinging chorus.

"Wait! You can't go—" The stage manager grabbed Johnny's black velvet sleeve, but the tall blond boy wrenched himself free and stalked out onto the stage.

"Hand over that guitar, you thief!" Johnny grabbed at the guitar as Stan stared at him in amazement.

Stan resisted, after his first surprise, and clung to the guitar. "Let go! Who said it was yours?" he demanded angrily.

"I can prove it!" Johnny shouted. "You stole it out of my car! And you stole the car, too!"

The audience was in an uproar as the two young men

shouted at each other and struggled for possession of the guitar.

Annette sat stricken and sick while Tonia and Lola were excitedly trying to hear what Stan and Johnny were arguing about. "Oh, why didn't I mind my own business!" she reproached herself. Then, as Chief Trujillo went hurrying down the aisle and up onto the stage, she rose quickly and started for the exit from the box. But Tonia grabbed her arm.

"Where are you going? You can't get mixed up in it, whatever it is! Please, Annette!" Tonia was holding onto her cousin determinedly. "People are beginning to stare at you!"

"But it's all my fault! I've got to explain!" Annette tried to shake off her hand, but Tonia wouldn't let go of her, and Annette finally had to sit down again.

Chief Trujillo was on stage with the two young men, trying to find out what it was all about and keep them apart. He yelled angrily, "Quiet! Both of you!" and when they stopped trying to get at each other, he listened first to Johnny, who accused Stan loudly, and then to Stan, who denied he had stolen either the guitar or Johnny's car.

By then, the audience was aware of what the argument

was about, and younger members of it were loudly taking sides, hoping to see a battle on the stage. "Sock 'im, Stan!" one shouted.

But when Chief Trujillo, grim-faced, took Stan by the arm and led him, still hanging onto the disputed guitar, out of sight behind the flimsy canvas scenery, the band struck up an excited version of a Sousa march.

And by the time they had concluded the selection, everything had quieted down again, and it was time for Johnny to sing "The Roving Gambler."

Annette, worried sick, had to sit through it. She was queen, and the queen had to hand out the prizes as the climax of the contest. But she was wishing that she were any place but there.

They liked Johnny's style. He had plenty of assurance. It made up for his rather ordinary singing voice. They gave him applause that was enthusiastic enough to make the judges give him first prize.

And Annette *had* to smile as she handed over the certificate that entitled him to the expensive record player and hi-fi set. But her heart wasn't in it, and the moment she had given out all the prizes, she slipped away from the royal box and pushed her way through the milling crowd to the spot where her uncle and aunt were getting into the family car.

"Uncle Genio! Please! I've got to tell you something, right away!"

"Tonia's calling you, dear. I think they're going to take pictures now!" Aunt Betta interrupted.

But Annette told her hastily, "They don't need me. This is lots more important!" She turned to her uncle again. "Uncle Genio, Stan didn't steal Johnny's guitar! I took it and lent it to him. He didn't even know it was Johnny's! As for the car, I parked it down the street for Johnny yesterday. Was—was it really stolen?"

Judge Bori nodded, frowning. "Explain yourself, child."

So she went on to tell them what had happened, and when she had finished, her uncle told her gravely, "I'd better tell Chief Trujillo about this at once. A serious injustice has been done to the Turner boy."

"I'll go with you," Annette said anxiously.

"It won't be necessary, my dear. There's no use advertising your part in it to the general public."

"You'd better go back to Tonia," Aunt Betta suggested, patting Annette's hand. "Uncle will take care of it all."

"If you don't mind," Annette told her, "I'd rather go home and wait to hear. I don't feel like listening to Johnny Abbott boast about winning the first prize when I know that if it hadn't been for my bungling, Stan would have won it. I've made him lose a chance for a career, just because I didn't speak up honestly about taking that guitar."

"Stop blaming yourself, dear. You had no idea that the car would be stolen and Johnny would never get your note," Aunt Betta said firmly. "It was just bad luck."

But Annette couldn't brush off her sense of guilt so lightly. She got into the car and went home with her aunt to wait for word from Judge Bori.

# 15 *Surprise*

"Better lie down and rest a while, dear," Aunt Betta advised Annette as they entered the cool, high-ceilinged front hallway of the Bori home. "You mustn't be tired at the dance tonight. We want you to look your prettiest, Queen Annette!" She kissed Annette on the cheek and shooed her upstairs to her room.

But Annette wasn't ready to rest. She changed into her everyday clothes and sat staring unhappily out the window, waiting for the telephone to bring word from Uncle Genio that he had straightened out everything for poor Stan.

She heard it ring at last, after what seemed like an hour. Aunt Betta's voice sounded happy at first, but a moment later, it had a worried note in it. Annette rushed down the stairs with her heart in her mouth.

"Was that Uncle Genio, Aunt Betta? Is everything cleared up about the guitar?" Aunt Betta was just hanging up the receiver.

"Yes, dear, to both questions!" Aunt Betta smiled at her eager face, but sobered a moment later and looked troubled.

"Then why look so solemn?" Annette demanded, her own happy smile of relief fading away.

"Your uncle says that the boy was released, with an apology, but his attitude was—unfortunate." She frowned. "He was quite rude to your uncle and angry with everyone in Lost Creek. He accused Chief Trujillo of persecuting him because his father is in prison. And then he rushed out without even a thank-you!"

Annette thought unhappily, And it's my fault.

"Chief Trujillo told your uncle that if the Turner boy makes the least bit of trouble for Johnny Abbott—or anyone else—over this thing, he'll arrest him for disturbing the peace!" Her aunt looked stern.

Annette turned suddenly and started for the door.

"Now where are you going, dear? Don't you think you'd better rest?" Aunt Betta asked.

"I just remembered something I want to take care of."
Annette smiled at her with an effort. "I'll be back."

She stopped long enough to put on a brimmed straw hat
with bright red lining that came down and tied pertly under
her chin. Then she ran out and down the steep porch steps
and to the garage.

Old Mike had just finished polishing the Monster, and
she stopped to tell him what a good job he had done. Then
she got in hastily and steered the little sports car down into
town.

The holiday crowds were as big as ever, and the Malt
Shop was filled with customers.

She was glad that she hadn't run into Johnny and Tonia
on her way to the shop. She didn't feel like talking to anyone else until she had made her peace with Stan.

But Stan was not behind the counter. Instead, to her aston-
ishment, Deke Jensen was elbow deep in foaming suds, per-
spiration running down his reddened face, as he tried to keep
up with the waitresses' demands for clean glasses.

"Hi!" Annette slid onto a stool in front of Deke.
"Where's Stan Turner?"

"Oh, hi, Queenie! Tonia and Johnny are looking all over
for you! They just left."

"I'll catch up with them later. Where's Stan?" Annette could see he was trying to avoid answering that question. "And what are *you* doing working here?"

"He quit," Deke answered defiantly. "Job was open, so I took it—for the rest of the day."

"Why did he quit?" Annette persisted over the noise all around them.

"Johnny and Tonia were here when Stan came back from the police station to go to work. Johnny made a mean crack, and Stan belted him."

Annette said, "Oh!" and closed her eyes. "Did Johnny have him arrested again?" She remembered what her aunt had told her the police chief had said to Uncle Genio about what would happen to Stan if he made any trouble.

"Nah! He knew he'd talked out of turn and had that sock in the nose coming."

"What did Johnny say to make Stan angry?"

"Hey, Nick's giving me the dog-eye. I'll get fired if you don't quit making me jabber." He got very busy rattling silver in the hot water. Nick was moving past, frowning.

When he had gone by, Deke looked up at Annette, who was waiting determinedly. "Why don't you ask Stan? He said he was going home to pack his things and get out of

Lost Creek for good. You ought to be able to catch up to him before he gets too far out of town, even if he walks fast."

"Thanks, Deke!" Annette hurried out through the tourist crowd and to her car on the side street.

"Annette! Hey, 'Nette!" Tonia, her pretty cheeks flushed, was hurrying toward the car, towing Johnny along behind her by the hand. Johnny was scowling and holding a handkerchief to his nose. "Wait!"

For a moment, Annette was tempted to pretend that she hadn't heard her cousin's voice, but she gave up the idea. Might as well face it, once and for all, she thought glumly, and waited in her car till they came up.

"Gosh, Annette! Where have you been? You ran off and I've been trying to find you ever since!"

"I was home, resting—for a while."

"Oh!" That seemed to satisfy Tonia. "Johnny wants to tell you something."

"Yes?" Annette waited coolly.

Johnny swallowed hard. Then, defiantly, he announced, "I talked to the committee. And they think it's only fair for me to lead the grand march tonight with you. I won the song contest, and that makes me the one you're *supposed* to choose to be Prince Charming."

Annette kept her face blank, but she turned to Tonia for her opinion. Tonia clutched Johnny's hand and smiled contentedly.

"It's all right with me, Annette," she said, flashing a quick smile at the sullen Johnny. "It's just that Johnny thinks it would be good publicity for him. You know, for his singing career when he starts making records."

Annette shrugged. "I haven't asked anybody else—yet. I'll see you both later."

And then, before either of them could say anything, she started the Monster's motor with a deafening roar and pulled out into the traffic, waving good-bye quite casually.

Johnny glared after her angrily. "She can't brush me off like that! I haven't told anybody that she stole my guitar for that Turner punk, but I will if she doesn't act reasonable."

Tonia stuck out her chin, and her blue eyes flashed. "She had a right to take it! She made a deal with you, and you went back on it first! And if you say one word about her 'stealing' your beaten-up old guitar, I'll never talk to you again!"

Johnny's scowl faded. He could see that Tonia meant what she had said. If Tonia dropped him, the gang would, too. It would be a pretty dismal summer.

"Okay! Okay! I was just letting off steam. I'm not going to say a word."

Tonia relaxed and patted his arm. "That's my boy!" She linked her arm with his. "And for being nice, I'm going to persuade her to choose you for Prince Charming tonight. Just wait and see!"

And they strolled through the crowd together, getting lots of attention as people recognized the song contest winner and the princess. Every few yards, they had to stop and pose for snapshots. All the tourists seemed to have cameras of one sort or another.

There was only one thing that spoiled Johnny's enjoyment of the publicity he was getting. So far, he had not heard from any representative of a record company. He had been told—as had the other contestants—that there'd be at least one talent scout at Lost Creek to judge the singing and perhaps sign the winner. But if there had been one, he hadn't come forward with a contract for Johnny. Not yet, anyhow. Perhaps he was waiting to make a big thing of it tonight at the Square Dance Ball!

Stan Turner's mother finished her day's work at the Lunchroom and wearily started for home. She had heard snatches of conversation during the afternoon, about Johnny Abbott winning the song contest, and she knew how Stan must be feeling.

She was unaware that Stan had been arrested and then released. The gossip hadn't reached the busy lunch counter.

As she hurried to catch the local bus that would take her home, she tried desperately to think of something consoling to say to Stan when she got there. Margie would need cheering up, too, poor little thing. She had been so sure that Stan couldn't lose!

Meanwhile, Annette drove out toward the Turner place, watching for Stan along the road. She rather dreaded facing him, but it was something that had to be done. She hoped he wouldn't be too angry and bitter.

As she crossed the covered bridge at the foot of Main Street, she saw Stan at the other end of the bridge, disappearing down the bank toward the creek. He was paying no attention to the approaching car.

She emerged from the darkness of the bridge and glanced down toward the creek. She saw that Stan was sitting on a rock close to the water, chin cupped in one hand as he stared at the tumbling rush of the stream.

Annette pulled up alongside the road in the first wide spot where she could park out of traffic, got out, and walked back toward the bridge.

As she reached the end of the bridge and began to take the small footpath down toward Stan, the local bus from town came through, rattling the bridge's old floor timbers.

In the fast-moving bus, Mrs. Turner stared out of her window and thought, That's odd! That girl back there looked like Judge Bori's niece. But it couldn't have been! Then she went back to worrying over what she could say to comfort her son for losing the contest.

Stan Turner stared at the water, but he wasn't seeing it. He was bitterly reliving the afternoon. His fists clenched as he thought of Johnny Abbott's public accusal of him, the disgrace of being arrested as a thief—

"Stan. . . ." For a moment, he thought that Annette's soft voice was only in his imagination. Then, as he turned his head, he saw her standing quite close, an appealing little smile on her lips and her hand held out to him. She was really there.

Stan rose abruptly, on guard against her friendly approach. He frowned defiantly at her, ignoring her hand.

"I'm sorry, Stan." Her hand dropped to her side. "I

don't blame you for being angry. All I was trying to do was help you. I knew you had to have that guitar."

"You should have told me it was his!" Stan said sharply. "I wouldn't have taken it for a minute!"

"I knew that," she said quietly, "or I would have told you."

"Oh, well, forget it! The silly contest is all over now, anyhow. I wouldn't have won."

"You would, too!" Annette contradicted him. "You were super!"

"You forget who I am . . . a convict's son. . . ." Stan sneered at himself. "Why would anybody in Lost Creek give me a prize? I had a lot of nerve even trying!"

Annette studied him silently. Stan's face reddened. He knew what she was thinking: that he was feeling sorry for himself again. Suddenly, he made a helpless gesture with his hands. "There I go again! Why do you bother?" And he turned away.

Annette herself wasn't quite sure what the answer was to that, so she didn't try to tell him.

"The way it adds up"—he stared moodily across the water—"the sooner I get out of Lost Creek and try to make a start where nobody knows what my father is supposed to have done, the better!"

"But where will you go? And how about your mother and Margie? Don't they need you here?" she asked quickly.

"They'd be better off someplace else, too. I'll send for them as soon as I find a steady job."

"Well," Annette said with a sigh, "I suppose nobody can tell you how to live your own life. But it seems to me you're running away from something that isn't there."

"Isn't there? You saw how fast they grabbed me and hauled me off to jail when Johnny Abbott called me a thief!" Stan looked grim. "Nobody believed I had borrowed that guitar. They all *wanted* to think that the convict's son was a thief!"

"Why didn't you tell them that *I* lent it to you? Why did you let them keep you in jail till Uncle Genio came and told them it was *my* fault?"

"I didn't want to drag your name into it after Johnny made such a scene in front of all those people."

"I wouldn't have minded. And there wouldn't have been all that fuss. And I bet you'd have won!"

Stan shrugged. "Thanks for the vote of confidence, but I know better." He smiled at her.

"Stubborn!" Annette shook her head. Then she had a

sudden thought. "Stan! If you're so set on leaving Lost Creek, why don't you try San Francisco? Uncle Genio has offices there, and he knows *everybody*. He'd be glad to find a good job for you. All you have to do is ask him."

Stan's smile faded. "No, thanks," he said stiffly. "I don't want any favors from Judge Bori."

Annette gave a little sigh. "That's right. I forgot for a minute how you feel about Uncle Genio. I'm sorry I brought it up." And she turned away and started up toward the road.

Stan looked after her with a baffled expression. "Thanks, anyway."

Annette stopped and looked back with a little smile. "You're welcome. And good luck, Mister Independent. I hope you get rich and famous!"

A wide grin spread across Stan's face. "I'll sure try my level best!"

Annette nodded, with an answering grin. "Meanwhile, could I give you a lift home?"

"Gosh, yes! If it isn't out of your way!" And a moment later, they were climbing up the pathway to the road and strolling toward Annette's car.

It seemed less than a minute to both of them before Annette turned off the highway onto the dirt road that led back toward the small Turner house and barn.

"Mom should be home by now. She usually gets the four o'clock bus from town." Stan got out of the little car slowly. "I'd sort of like her to hear what really happened this afternoon. She's probably heard all sorts of gossip at the Lunchroom."

"I'd be glad to see her again—and Margie, too." Annette opened the door on her side and got out.

"She likes you," Stan said, a little shyly, as they moved up the path toward the small fenced yard.

When they were still a dozen feet away, Mrs. Turner opened the front door and stepped out. She closed the door behind her and came hurriedly toward them, a strained look on her face.

Annette's friendly greeting died in her throat at the sight of Mrs. Turner's stern expression.

"Something wrong, Mom?" Stan asked quickly.

"Of course not!" Mrs. Turner spoke sharply. "But I'm sure Miss McCleod will excuse us if we don't ask her in. There's something I must talk over with you."

"Oh, that's all right, Mrs. Turner," Annette assured her

hastily. "I must get right back to town anyhow. I'll see you later, Stan."

"But—" Stan frowned. This wasn't like his mother. "Annette and I want to tell—"

"You can do it without me!" Annette said. And then she turned quickly and hurried back toward her car.

Stan looked after her and then turned to his mother. "What's the score, Mom? I suppose you blame her for what happened in the contest? Well, it wasn't Annette's fault—"

Behind them, Annette's motor roared and a moment later they heard her driving away.

A voice, harsh and unfriendly, called out from somewhere beyond the open window of the little house. "Get in here, both of you. Now!"

# 16 *The Intruder*

Stan didn't recognize the rough voice that called out to him and his mother from inside their home.

"Who's that?" he asked his mother anxiously. "What's going on, Mom?"

"It's someone who knows your father. Let's go in." His mother hurried him toward the house.

"Why is he giving orders?" Stan demanded, holding back. "Who is he?"

"Come in and find out, sonny!" The denim-clad, black-bearded man who opened the door and stood looking out at them with a sneer on his twisted lips was no one that Stan had ever seen before. "Get in here!"

"Do as he says," his mother whispered. Her hand,

clutching Stan's arm, was shaking. "He might hurt you."

The bearded man in the doorway had a chunk of bread in one hand and a cold chicken leg in the other. He took a hungry bite of the chicken as he stepped out of the way to let them enter. "Sit down!" he ordered, with his mouth full. When Stan held back, scowling at him, the man grabbed Stan's arm with his greasy hand and spun the tall boy across the room toward the table. "Sit down, I said!"

"Please, Stan!" Mrs. Turner's eyes were wide with fear. "Mr. Martin is a friend of Dad's. He's been waiting all afternoon for us."

Stan sat down, but he kept his eyes on Martin. "Did Dad send you?" He could hardly believe his father would have anything to do with a man of Martin's type.

"Sure, sonny! He told me what a swell family he had, down here in Lost Creek. An' he said they'd do anything fer a friend of their pa's!" He finished the chicken hungrily and stuffed the last bite of the bread into his mouth. "So I come!" He reached for another slice of bread, but he dropped it again as the sound of a noisy old automobile engine came in through the open window.

Martin's hand streaked under his dirty denim jacket,

and Stan saw that he had a pistol stuck in his belt. "Who's that?" the black-bearded man snarled.

Mrs. Turner hurried to the window to peer out. "It's only my little girl, Margie. The neighbors down the road took her to the singing contest and are bringing her home."

"Get rid of them and bring her in here," he ordered grimly, his hand still touching the revolver in his belt.

But as Mrs. Turner started toward the door, they all heard the shouted good-byes between Margie and another little girl, and then the diminishing racket of the old motor as the car backed out toward the highway again.

"Please—don't frighten her! Stan and I will do anything you want us to do, but, please, don't scare my baby!" Mrs. Turner pleaded, as Margie's running steps came up the garden walk.

"Hey, I got kids o' my own! She an' me will get along swell, if you two watch yourselves!" He closed the denim coat so that the revolver was hidden and sat down again at the table. "Get me some more chow. I'm still hungry. An' you, kid"—he glowered at Stan—"just do like I tell you, an' you won't get hurt. So don't try to sneak out. I'm keepin' my eye on you."

Margie came in hurriedly. "Stan! We went to the police

station to see you, but—" She suddenly noticed the bearded stranger seated at the table and finished the rest of the sentence slowly and with her eyes on Martin, "but they said they'd already let you go because you hadn't done anything."

Stan nodded. "Yeah. I'm out."

Martin laughed. "Hi, Margie! My name's Jim Martin, and your pa said for me to give you his love."

Margie's eyes brightened and she ran to the table. "When's he coming home? Did they find out he didn't kill that old man?"

Mrs. Turner sat rigid and tense, and Stan hoped fervently that the bearded man's good humor would last.

"Well, now, they're gettin' to it!" He winked aside to Mrs. Turner. "It won't be long before you see him."

"Were you in prison, too?" Margie sat down and looked soberly at Martin.

"Sure! I helped run it! But I got tired of the same old thing every day, so I decided to take a vacation. And here I am."

"Vacation?" Margie asked. "Fishing and hunting like Dad used to do up in the High Sierras?"

"Somethin' like that," he said with a chuckle, helping

himself to the last of the fresh green onions standing in the glass holder on the table. "Say! I could eat some more of these! You wanna pick me a few in the garden?"

"I'll get them for you," said Mrs. Turner, rising quickly.

"Uh-uh!" Martin shook his head. "I want to talk to you about somethin'. Here!" He handed the empty glass to Margie. "Run along, kid. Pick some nice young ones."

"Sure!" Margie ran out happily.

Martin came to the point at once. "I've got to get out of here as soon as it's dark. I figure to head for a cabin your husband used to talk about, up at some lake. Loon Lake, he called it." He turned to Stan. "You know your way?"

"Yeah."

"Figured you would. Well, you can show me."

"We don't have a car. It's two hours from here."

"*I* got the car. Picked it up when some little dame parked it with the keys in it yesterday. Me an' the car hid out in one of them ghost towns, place called Applejack, down the road. Too many tourists snoopin' around there, so this afternoon when the law and everybody else was at some singin' shindig, I moved it to your barn. It's hid out there now, waitin' till dark."

Stan had a sudden hunch. "Is it a big blue car—a convertible?"

"Yeah! How'd you guess?"

"I know it's missing. And I wouldn't drive it for a million dollars!" Stan said defiantly.

Martin's face looked threatening. "*I'm* drivin' it. But you're goin' along to show me the way. And if you try any tricks, you ain't comin' back." He turned to Mrs. Turner, who had listened white-faced and helpless. "And if you send the law after us, the same goes. You don't see the kid here again. Understand?"

She nodded mutely. Stan looked rebellious, but he remembered the gun, and he had no more to say.

Margie ran in, eagerly displaying the freshly gathered green onions. "Aren't they nice? They're from my very own garden. I'll fix 'em up for you."

"That's the girl! You fix 'em, I'll eat 'em!"

And while Margie was washing and trimming the long green sprouts, he sat at ease, grinning maliciously at mother and son.

"It's pretty cold up at the lake, even this time of year," Stan ventured.

"That's how I like it," his captor replied. "We'll take

plenty of blankets. And your mom here will pack us some of them cans of food I see up there on the shelf." He motioned to Mrs. Turner to get up and start packing her supply of beans, canned corn, and tomatoes in a carton. When she hesitated after taking down a dozen or so cans, he said, "Go ahead. We got good appetites. Ain't we, kid?"

And when Stan didn't answer, he laughed and slapped Stan on the back so hard that he almost knocked him out of his chair. Stan's fists clenched, but he restrained himself because his mother looked terrified and shook her head vigorously in warning.

Margie ran over from the sink with the green onions. "Here you are, Mr. Martin!"

"Thanks, sister!" and he began gobbling one after the other, only pausing to shake salt on each before popping it into his mouth and chewing noisily.

Margie looked at him with a doubtful expression. She was trying to like this friend of her father's, but he certainly had terrible table manners! And neither Stan nor Mother seemed to be glad to have him around.

When the onions were gone and all the bread had disappeared from the table, Jim Martin pushed back his chair.

"Well, now. I feel a mite better. All set to travel!" He went to the window and peered out. The sun was still above the Sierra foothills. "We'll pull out, soon as it gets a mite darker." He stood staring out.

"You must eat something, too," Mrs. Turner told Stan.

"Not hungry." Stan shook his head.

"Better eat your ma's cookin' while you can," Martin said with a coarse laugh. "You may be eatin' your own for quite a spell!"

"How long are you and Stan going to be away on your vacation?" Margie asked, puzzled.

"That's kinda up to Stan, sis!" The words were innocent enough, but both Mrs. Turner and Stan knew that Martin was repeating his warning not to put the law on their trail. "Now, how about gettin' some blankets and stuff?"

So they moved about under his watchful eye and got ready to pack the car as soon as it was dark enough outside.

Annette had driven directly home after leaving Stan at the little house off the highway. She couldn't help believing that Mrs. Turner's coldness was because of the disastrous guitar incident and Stan's loss of the contest prize as a result of it.

"I don't blame her," she told herself unhappily. "Little Miss Fix-it certainly did a great job messing up that boy's life! If only there were something I could do to make it up to Stan!"

But she couldn't think of a thing.

She put the Monster away in the Bori garage and went into the house. Tonia met her in the hallway.

"Mother's on the warpath! She says we've both got to rest for tonight! Where've you been?"

"Just—out," Annette told her carelessly as they started up the stairs together.

"I can hardly wait for tonight! Can you?" Tonia babbled.

"I don't feel too awfully good. I think I have a headache or something coming on." Annette really didn't feel like going to a dance.

"Oh, you're just tired! You'll feel fine after you rest a couple of hours." They were at Annette's bedroom door. "Hustle in there now and relax!"

"Tone"—Annette looked serious—"if I don't feel any better this evening, will you do me a favor?"

"Why, of course!" Tonia told her promptly. "What?"

"Will you take my place as queen for the dance?"

"Gracious! I can't do *that*. What would people say? They'd think I took it back from you!"

"No, they wouldn't! Not if Uncle Genio and Aunt Betta let the committee know that I don't feel well."

Tonia tried to keep the excitement of the prospect of being queen from showing on her pretty face, but it was a lost effort. In spite of herself, her eyes were dancing. But she still made a valiant effort. "You'll feel lots better when you've had a nap."

"Well, I'll try." Annette sighed. Then, as she started into her room, she said, "Oh, I forgot to phone Johnny Abbott that he'll be Prince Charming. Will you take care of it for me?"

"Right away!" Tonia smiled happily. "He'll be so glad to hear it. He even thought you might choose that Stan Turner, though I told him the committee would never stand for it, even if you did!" She hugged Annette suddenly, and a moment later she was hurrying downstairs to phone him.

Annette closed the door and went to stretch out across her bed, deep in thought. At least, she thought, she could make Tonia happy. And the dance and being queen didn't seem to mean a thing to her now anyhow. Her heart, in one of Aunt Lila's favorite expressions, wasn't in it. She was suffering from an attack of conscience because Stan Turner had lost his chance to win the singing contest. She could imagine how bad he must be feeling right this very minute!

Annette was right about how Stan Turner was feeling just then. But his feelings had nothing to do with the contest he had lost.

He was desperately trying to think of some way that he could outguess the dark-browed man who sat leering at him and his mother as they packed their few blankets into bedrolls at his command. But there was that revolver in Jim Martin's belt—and Stan's growing realization that even if he did manage to escape, by some trick, his mother and sister might be the next hostages to be carried off by the runaway convict.

As darkness fell over Lost Creek, the lights of most of the small houses went on, but in the Turner home the curtains were closely drawn so that the lamplight wouldn't shine out and perhaps seem to invite some of their neighbors to drop in.

Soon it was completely dark outside. Little Margie, tired out by the excitement of the long day, had long since dropped off to sleep and been put to bed by her mother. After her first effort, the child had made no more friendly overtures to the dark stranger. As children often do, Margie had sensed that there was something about Jim Martin to be feared, although her mother had cheerfully assured her it was only his manners that were rough.

At Martin's orders, Stan opened the old barn doors and backed the big convertible out into the open. He glanced at the registration certificate that Martin had not even bothered to remove, and saw that, as he had guessed, it was Johnny Abbott's car! If anyone saw him riding in that car, no amount of talking would convince the police that he hadn't stolen it yesterday.

But Stan had no choice. After he had loaded the food and blankets, he got harsh orders from Jim Martin to "kiss your ma, and let's go."

"Don't worry, Mom. I'll be back soon," he told her, kissing her gently.

"I know you will!" she told him bravely.

Martin got into the car from the other side. "Just don't forget what I said, Miz' Turner! You send the law up there looking for me, an' you've seen the last of this young 'un! Okay, boy. Hit the road!"

And a minute later, the big car had lumbered out of the narrow driveway and onto the deserted highway, disappearing into the darkness in the direction of Loon Lake.

# 17 *The Captive*

Many times during the next hour, Mrs. Turner was tempted to disobey Jim Martin's harsh orders and go to the police with her story, but each time she stopped, realizing bitterly that there could be no doubt that the desperate man would carry out his threat to get rid of Stan if the law followed them.

But there would be no sleep for her that night, and she had to remember to keep up the pretense to Margie that Jim Martin and Stan had merely gone for a few days of hunting and fishing. She prayed that she wouldn't break down and let the child see how terribly frightened she was.

At the Bori mansion on the hill above town, Tonia

tiptoed out of her room and down the hallway to Annette's. She listened for a hint of movement inside, and when everything remained quiet, she carefully opened the door and peered into the dark room.

"Come on in, Tone!" Annette's voice came softly from over by the window. "Please don't switch on the light! It makes my headache worse."

Tonia exclaimed sympathetically and hurried to her cousin. "Oh! You haven't started to dress yet!"

"I'm not going to the dance. I don't feel like it at all. You'll have to stand in for me."

"I'm so sorry. Is there anything we can do for you? I'd better call Mother." And before Annette could stop her, she had sped out of the room and hurried downstairs to the dinner table, where her father and mother were waiting for both girls.

Aunt Betta hurried up to Annette's room at once, full of sympathy and carrying her pet headache remedy.

"I'll be all right, Aunt Betta. I'm just overtired, I guess." She accepted the headache pills meekly and promised to take more of them during the evening if the first ones didn't work.

An hour later, she heard Katey answering the doorbell

and the sound of voices in the lower hall. She recognized one of them as Johnny's. She smiled, catching the note of happy excitement in his voice as he playfully congratulated Tonia on her appearance.

Tonia, her parents, and Johnny left a few minutes later in the Bori car. Annette watched them drive off, and then she sat back and relaxed. I hope Tonia has a perfectly wonderful time, she thought. I couldn't have gone through it, I know!

And she spent the next couple of hours writing a happy letter to Aunt Lila and Uncle Archie, telling them all sorts of amusing little things about the celebration and carefully avoiding any details that might worry them.

Then she went to bed, wondering how it would have seemed if she had kept the queen title and had been permitted to choose Stan Turner to be Prince Charming.

Maybe it's just as well this way, she thought sleepily after a while. He's tall and I'm such a shorty. People might have laughed. And the next moment, she was sound asleep.

But Stan Turner was too busy right then to be thinking of anything except keeping the heavy car on the rain-swept road that led up into the high mountains. The previous night's heavy rain had left deep mudholes at the edges of the road, and a driving shower was making the road slippery and dangerous. It was slow going.

Once they had gotten well out of the populated area, the tired convict had insisted on Stan's taking the wheel.

"But no tricks, sonny," he had warned. "Just keep on going till you get there."

The sudden heavy shower had soaked them both before Stan had managed to find the button that raised the top over them and kept out the rain.

"Hope the road isn't washed out," Stan muttered over the rhythmic buzzing of the windshield wipers. But he got no answer from Jim Martin. The convict was asleep.

I could stop here, get out, and make a run for it, Stan thought, keeping his eyes on the curtain of rain that hid everything but the nearest few yards of road.

But when he gradually let the motor slow down, Martin awoke with a start, his hand moving toward the gun in his belt. He sat up, glaring around menacingly. "What is it? Why are we stopping?" he demanded.

"Can't see more than twenty feet. Had to slow down," Stan told him hastily, and was relieved to see his black-bearded captor slump down in his seat again. Stan thought grimly, I better not try that. He sleeps with one eye open, like a cat. And he reaches for that gun pretty fast!

So they crawled on through the darkness and rain, the big car swaying and skidding on muddy turns. At last, after what seemed a century, the rain slackened and then stopped entirely. Suddenly, there was a roadside sign that said LOON LAKE RESORT—2 MILES, and pointed a jagged finger toward a cutoff road. Stan stopped the car.

"Almost there," Stan told Martin, as the convict stirred and yawned.

Martin squinted at the road sign, lit by the car's head-lights. "Two miles, huh? What's this 'resort'? Your pa didn't say there was a settlement!" He scowled un-easily.

"Nothing there anymore," Stan told him. "Empty shacks. Used to be a mining camp years ago. Then real estaters tried to build it up as a summer resort. But it was too far off the main road."

"Good! We don't want company! Might make you for-get to keep your mouth shut, an' that wouldn't be so good—for Ma and Pa Turner's little feller!" He laughed.

Stan felt goose pimples up and down his spine. Martin might laugh, but he meant what he said!

"What's stalling us? Let's move!" Martin growled. "We don't wanna run into anybody that'll remember us."

"There's probably nobody in five miles," Stan told him as he started the big car up the cutoff road.

But there *was* somebody else there. A stooped old man with a white beard watched them from behind the rain-drenched brush. His blue eyes burned with anger under bushy brows. "Drat it! Why can't a man git some peace an' quiet?" he muttered, shaking his fist at the big car turning into the steep-angled road. "Noise an' smell, everywhere I go! Wisht I had me a rifle! I'd bust open their fancy white-sided tires for them dudes! Teach 'em to stay off my mountain!" And he glared after the car till the sound of its motor died away.

After a series of turns and twists in the narrow rough road, they reached an old cabin in a clearing that overlooked a small lake many hundred feet below.

"We're here," Stan said wearily.

"Pull in close to the shack and start unloadin'," Martin ordered.

Stan pulled up almost to the front door, and Martin

got out. "Keep the lights on. I'll take a look around inside."

He stopped suddenly, staring at the ground, his hand going to his gun. The headlights showed that the weeds that grew almost up to the shack had been trampled down in a sort of pathway to the door. He bent over and examined the ground. Then he picked up a handful of grass.

"Still green. Somebody's been around in the last day or so." He was whispering, keeping his hand close to the butt of his revolver. "Might be asleep in there now!"

"Probably some fisherman getting out of the rain," Stan answered in the same low tone. "Shall I give him a yell?"

"Nah!" Martin scowled. He drew his revolver and moved stealthily up to the door. He kicked it with all his strength and it creaked open. It hadn't even been latched. Martin jumped aside, out of a possible line of fire from whoever was in there, but nothing happened.

The car lights shone into an empty cabin. After a moment, Martin decided that it was safe to go inside. He moved slowly through the doorway and disappeared inside. Stan heard him trip over something and exclaim angrily.

Stan had a sudden inspiration. This might be his chance

to get away from his captor. He wheeled and ran back to the car.

But one glance at the dashboard revealed that Martin had taken the key from the ignition. The convict was one jump ahead of his young captive. "Why didn't I have brains enough to pocket it?" Stan asked himself angrily. "What a dope!"

"Hey, kid! Cart them blankets and the grub in here!" Martin called from the shack. "Don't take all night!"

Stan picked up the heavy carton of canned food and staggered toward the shack with it. Poor Mom! he thought. All her homemade jelly and stuff!

Someone had occupied the old cabin not too long ago. There were ashes in the fireplace and a faint smell of broiled fish in the air. A half-burned candle stood on a shelf, with a shriveled potato for a candlestick.

There were many boot marks on the dirt floor, and even some half-dried mud that had been tracked in by those same boots.

Spiderwebs were festooned across the low ceiling, and both Martin and Stan had to duck their heads to avoid getting tangled in their dusty lengths. They had evidently hung there for a year or more.

A rough pine table and a bench were at one side of the small room, and there was a single bunk across from the fireplace, with a musty old piece of canvas stretched across the ropes that did duty as springs.

But the one thing that proved someone had been there very recently was the tin dish lying on the table, holding a half-eaten baked potato and the backbone of what must have been a trout from the lake.

Martin took up the plate and handed it to Stan. "Out!" he ordered. "And lug in them blankets before it starts to rain again."

It took several trips, but Stan finally got everything in and the car lights turned off. He was tired enough by then to think of turning in and leaving the problem of escape till morning.

Martin was sitting on the edge of the only bunk, taking off his shoes, when Stan put up the bar across the door. He saw the boy look around inquiringly and guessed what he was thinking. "What's eatin' yuh now, kid?" He grinned a twisted grin. "Scared yuh'll catch cold sleepin' on the floor?" he jeered. "Fine Boy Scout you musta been!"

Stan didn't answer, though his trigger temper flared. He

told himself silently, Watch it, bud! Get along with him till you can figure out how to get away.

So he managed to grin at Martin as he spread out a couple of blankets and wrapped them around him till he looked like an oversized papoose.

Then he hobbled over to the wooden bench beside the table and gingerly lay down along it. The bench wasn't more than a foot and a half wide, and less than six feet long, but it was a lot better than lying on the floor, where spiders, rats, and other assorted wildlife probably roamed in the dark hours of the night. Just hope I don't fall off, he thought, as the last end of the candle sputtered out in its potato candlestick.

The bench was hard, and Martin was beginning to snore heavily. "I could try to get away now," Stan told himself sleepily, but he was too warm in the good wool blankets and too exhausted after the long, long day to move.

In a few minutes, he was dead to the world, and he lay like a log all night in spite of Martin's snores.

Along toward dawn, Jim Martin awoke suddenly and lay listening, his hand on the revolver lying beside his shoulder. He was sure he had heard something.

He raised himself on his elbow, gun ready, and stared at the door. It was closed tight, and there was no sound of anything stirring in the room.

But the runaway convict was not satisfied. He pushed back his blankets and swung his feet to the floor. Gun in hand, he moved soundlessly past the sleeping young man to the door.

The bar that Stan had fixed across the door was still firmly held in the iron sockets at the sides of the doorway. No one could have come in.

Martin thought suddenly of the stolen car standing out in the open. Whoever was prowling around out there might recognize that car or might read the owner's name on the registration slip. The police must have a bulletin out by now for the stolen car.

Well, there was one way to keep the snooper from running to the law!

He carefully lifted the wooden bar and opened the door, gun in hand.

In the bright moonlight, he saw that there was no one in the clearing. But as his eyes swept over the brush, he saw movement. Something like the shape of a man was disappearing into the thicket. In a flash, it was gone.

Grimly, he circled the clearing, staying in the shadows of the trees that rimmed it.

Now he could hear the movement in the thicket, the sound of breaking twigs as something passed through. He stood motionless, locating the sound. Then, with his revolver leveled, he moved stealthily toward it.

He advanced a few feet more, a few inches at a time, as the sound of movement grew more distinct. He released the safety catch on his gun.

Then he got a look at the intruder. It was an ancient gray burro, trailing a broken lead rope. The animal was grazing a small patch of grass between the manzanita bushes. It lifted its head and stared at him for a long moment, while Martin stared back. Then it calmly went back to eating the grass.

For a moment, Martin was tempted to shoot the disturber of his sleep. His finger tightened on the trigger. Then he shook his head. "Nah! You look like you run away, same as me!" he said softly. And he stuck the gun into his belt and went back to the cabin.

But before he fell asleep again, Martin made up his mind to get rid of the big car in the morning. "We can hide out a lot safer without it!" he said to himself. And before the supplies ran out, he could pick up another car and move on. He felt sure Mrs. Turner would keep quiet about his whereabouts, for Stan's sake.

She'd better, he thought—or else.

# 18 *Annette's Errand*

Several hours later, the bright Sierra sun was pouring through the open door of the old cabin as Stan Turner awoke.

For a moment, he didn't know where he was and stared around in a daze. Then he remembered and sat up abruptly. There was a familiar sound coming from somewhere outside—the deep roaring of a powerful motor. Someone was gunning the cold car engine.

He staggered to the doorway and peered out, blinking. He was just in time to see Jim Martin backing the car away from the cabin, turning it, and then heading directly toward the thick brush. He watched, too surprised to move, expecting that at any second, the convict would swing the car toward the road and drive off. He must have changed his mind about sticking around up here, Stan thought happily. Looks like he's leaving.

But Jim Martin had other plans. He had discovered that a thickly wooded ravine lay at the foot of that side of the mountain, an ideal hiding place for even as large an object as the stolen car. He gunned the motor as he came closer to the manzanita thicket, waited till the last moment, then jumped out of the fast-moving car!

It smashed its way through the brush and disappeared. A moment later Stan heard a series of crashes as the heavy car struck the rocky sides of the mountain on its way down.

Martin started back to the cabin and saw Stan in the doorway. "That's one they'll have a tough time finding!" he boasted.

Before Stan could reply, there was an explosion, far below in the ravine.

"That fixes that!" Martin grinned. "Now, how's about breakfast?" He saw Stan staring at the thicket. "What's on your mind?" he demanded.

"Fire," Stan told him.

Martin shrugged. "Too wet. But if we see any smoke,

we'll have plenty of time to hike out before the fire gets up here." And as Stan still looked doubtful, Martin scowled. "Forget it. Hustle up some grub."

When an hour passed without any spiral of smoke rising from the deep ravine, Stan realized that Martin had been right. Possibly it was the wetness, after the torrential rains of the last couple of days. Then again, it might have been because there was very little gas left in the big car to spread a fire. Whatever the cause was, Stan was glad. Getting off that mountain might have been an impossibility once a fire had started.

Just out of sight, on a hillside above the shack, the old prospector squatted in front of the small timbered entrance of an abandoned mine. Inside, his breakfast fire was still smoldering, and his two burros were nodding sleepily at the end of their ropes.

Chico, the gray smaller one, had chewed his lead rope apart some time during the night, and his master had searched from dawn to sunrise for the rascal. Chico was now dozing peacefully, with a stomach full of grass, none the worse for his excursion. But the old prospector was cross and tired. Cross at the burro and at the two men who had moved into the old shack. It wasn't much of a place, but he had planned to use it himself. He pondered how he could get them out of there so he could move in. But no ideas came.

After a while, he gave up and went into the tunnel with his pick and shovel to do some digging where, years ago perhaps, some other miner had pecked away hopefully at the mountain and then had given up hope and departed for new prospects.

He had been inside the old tunnel, sizing up the loose ore scattered on the floor, when he had heard the crashing fall of the big car. The explosion that had followed had brought him running out to calm the two burros, who were in a wild panic of kicking and trying to break their ropes.

For a moment, it seemed as if Chico would be loose again, but the prospector finally managed to calm the gray beast. In the still air, he could hear the two men's voices below, but not what they were saying. Mebbe they got a newfangled way of huntin', he thought. "Blow up a half a dozen deer at once. Hogs, that's what they are! Grab a man's cabin, kill off the game!" he grumbled to himself. "Too bad they didn't blow their own selves up!"

\* \* \*

Annette woke slowly in her room in the Bori mansion at Lost Creek. She had slept very well, though she hadn't expected to. Tonia had wanted to wake her the night before, to report all about the dance and what a wonderful time she and Johnny had enjoyed there. But her mother had sternly shooed her off to bed.

Annette sat up, rubbing her eyes and yawning out loud. Bright sunlight was streaming in the window, and she knew it must be long past breakfast time.

Then she heard agitated whispering in the hallway outside her door. She smiled and called out, "I'm awake! Come in, Tone!"

Even before she got the words out completely, the door flew open and Tonia popped in, carrying an armful of long-stemmed white roses tied with a huge silver ribbon that read PIONEER DAYS QUEEN.

"Look what the committee sent you! It just came!" She was happily excited. "They were so sorry you weren't feeling well last night! And everyone missed you. And tonight at the Box Social they want us to be twin queens and give out the prizes for the best dancers! Won't that be *super*?"

"Why, that's a lovely idea! Twin queens! That should be fun!"

"Everyone thinks so! And Johnny can sit between us!" Tonia clasped her hands and rolled her eyes heavenward. "Johnny says he bets the city papers will run a story about it. It'll be wonderful publicity for his career."

"Uh-huh." Annette nodded, but without much enthusiasm. "That reminds me. Which record company signed him?"

"Why—uh—" Tonia frowned a little. "So far he hasn't heard anything. We don't even know if any of them sent a scout. Seems funny, doesn't it?"

"I don't know." Annette thought she *did* know, but there was no use letting Tonia know that she didn't think much of Johnny's singing. "Maybe they'll write to him."

Tonia's face brightened. "I hadn't thought of that. Why, that must be it! I guess whoever the man was who came to the contest, he probably had to report back to the office before he said anything."

Katey poked her head into the room. "You feelin' good enough to eat downstairs, or do you want me to bring up a tray, Miss Annette?"

"Why, thanks, Katey! I feel all right. I'll be down in fifteen minutes, hungry as a wolf!"

But when she got to the table, she didn't feel very

hungry, after all. The newspaper that Uncle Genio had been reading at his breakfast lay near her plate, and she couldn't miss the front-page story on the mix-up about the borrowed guitar at the song contest. The reporter treated the incident as comic and hinted that it was a pretty girl who had caused it, but he named no names and called her "Miss X."

Very funny! she thought bitterly. Miss X—X standing for stupid! And she wondered if poor Stan had left town yet. If I could only make it up to him and his family some-how, she thought.

She heard the telephone ringing and Tonia running to answer it in the study. Tonia's voice came clearly, "Oh! Deke?" She evidently had expected it to be Johnny. "She's eating breakfast. Do you want to call back?"

Annette got up and hurried across the hall to the library. "I'm through eating, Tone. Is it for me?"

Tonia nodded indifferently and handed the receiver to her. "Says it's important!" she whispered with a sniff. "Big shot!"

"Hi, Deke!" Annette liked Deke and Tim a lot better than she did Tonia's crush, Johnny. "What gives so early in the morn?" she challenged cheerfully.

"It's about Stan Turner!" Deke's voice sounded excited. "Do you know his number? It isn't in the phone book, and this dumb central says the Turners don't have one."

"I know they don't," Annette told him. "Is something wrong?"

"Anything but! Mr. Bradley of Astral Records was just in, wanting to talk to him. He wouldn't say, but I've got a big fat hunch he's decided to give Stan a tryout for his company. Boy, that's a big outfit!"

"Wonderful!" Annette was delighted.

"Yeah, only there's a catch," Deke explained. "Stan's got to get in touch with him right away, this afternoon. Mr. Bradley has to start back to the city around four o'clock."

"His mother works at the Star Lunchroom. She can tell him where to find Stan," Annette said eagerly.

"I sent him there," Deke told her soberly, "but she took one look at Mr. Bradley's card and told him that she was sure Stan wasn't interested in singing, after the way he was treated yesterday."

"But I *know* he would be! It's what he wants to do!" Annette protested.

"That's how I figure it, too!" Deke agreed. "But Mrs.

Turner wouldn't even give Mr. Bradley their address so he could go out and talk to Stan. She was all upset."

"I guess she has a right to be angry," Annette agreed glumly, "but it doesn't seem fair not to let Stan decide for himself whether he wants to talk to Mr. Bradley."

"Check! And if anybody around the Malt Shop here knew where the Turners live, we'd find someone to send to their place to tell Stan."

"I don't know how to tell you just which house it is, but I can find it easily," Annette said eagerly. "I'd be glad to go."

"Good gal! That's swell of you, Annette. Just pop by this morning if you can, and tell him Mr. Bradley's at the old Fremont Hotel on Hill Street. But he's leaving at five minutes to four, so Stan'd better be there!"

"I'll have him there at *ten* minutes to four at the latest!" Annette assured him with a confident laugh.

"You'll have who? Where? And why?" Tonia teased her as Annette turned from the phone after a hasty good-bye.

"Gracious! Did you overhear?" Annette pretended to be fainting. "You must keep my terrible secret. . . . I'm eloping with a lion tamer. . . . We're running away to Borneo!"

She ran to the front door, snatched up her purse and hat, threw a kiss back to Tonia, and was gone before Tonia recovered from her giggles.

"Who was that slamming the front door?" Judge Bori poked his head out of the library.

"Just Annette!" Tonia caroled back at him, taking the stairway two steps at a time. "She's eloping with a tame lion or something!" And she disappeared into her bedroom upstairs, singing "Here Comes the Bride" at the top of her voice.

"Goodness! What was all that about?" Mrs. Bori came in from talking to Katey in the kitchen about the lunch menu.

Judge Bori sighed and shook his head. "Something about Annette taking up lion taming, I think." And he went back into the library, closing the door firmly after him.

"Lion taming!" his wife echoed faintly. She hurried to the front door and stepped out onto the porch.

Annette backed her little white sports car out of the garage. She started past the house on the curved driveway and saw her aunt watching her anxiously. She waved merrily—"Bye, Aunt Betta!"—and then she was gone.

For the first time in twenty-four hours, Annette felt

thoroughly happy. She hummed snatches of "The Blue Juniata" as the little car sped along. At last she had a chance to do something to make it up to Stan for causing him to lose the contest!

She could just picture Stan's happy face when he heard that Mr. Bradley of Astral Records was anxious to talk to him.

It seemed only a minute or two before she was clear of town and approaching the dirt driveway that led off the highway and back to the Turner place.

Everything seemed very quiet as she stopped the car and got out. But when she pushed open the creaky little white gate in the garden fence, she saw Margie peeking out from behind the window curtains.

"Hi, Margie!" she called, and waved.

Margie's face disappeared, and a moment later the door opened. "Hi, Miss McCleod!" Margie's grin was as friendly as ever. "Mom's working, and Stan had to go away. But you can come in if you'd like to." And she looked as if she hoped Annette would accept the invitation.

"Why, thank you, Margie!" Annette was disappointed to hear Stan wasn't there, but she hoped he was just on an

errand somewhere. "I'll come in a minute. But I've got some news for Stan, if you'll tell me where to find him."

"Golly, I don't know where he went." Margie ran ahead of Annette into the little living room to clear off a chair for her guest. "Sit down and I'll make some tea."

"No, thanks, dear. I just had breakfast," Annette replied. "Are you expecting Stan back soon this morning?"

"Goodness, no! They've gone for a vacation. Up in the mountains." Margie was running around, clearing breakfast cups and saucers off the table and piling them in the sink.

"A vacation?" Annette looked alarmed. "For how long?"

"I dunno," Margie said, shaking her head.

"Did he say where?" Annette persisted.

"I'm not sure. They were talking about Loon Lake before I went to bed. I guess they went to the cabin there."

"Was it a hunting party? Is Stan guiding it?"

"No, it was just Mr. Martin—" She stopped suddenly and looked guilty, clapping her hand over her mouth.

"What's the matter?"

"Mom said not to tell about Mr. Martin. Please, don't

tell her I told you!" Margie seemed almost frightened. "She said something terrible would happen if I told anybody about Stan going with Mr. Martin."

"Of course I won't tell her—or anybody else! All I want to do is tell Stan some good news and take him to talk to the record-company man."

"The record company?" Margie's eyes sparkled and she clasped her hands together in delight. "Is he going to hire Stan?"

"I think so! I mean, I certainly feel sure he wouldn't want to talk to him right away if he didn't intend to give him an audition!" Annette assured her happily.

"Goody! Goody!" Margie jumped up and down and turned a cartwheel across the small room.

"But I've got to get Stan back to Lost Creek before four o'clock this afternoon to talk to the man!" Annette looked at her watch. "It's almost noon. How far is it to Loon Lake?"

"Just a couple of hours, I think. Maybe a little more. The gas station man can tell you."

"Thanks, hon! I'm off to Loon Lake with my fur flying in the breeze! See you later!" And she hurried out.

Margie ran after the car, waving and calling good-bye,

until Annette had backed it into the highway and driven off with a wave of her hand.

"Wish I coulda gone with her," Margie said with a sigh, as she went back into the house.

But of course, it was just as well she hadn't!

# 19 *Loon Lake*

Driving back through Lost Creek, Annette smiled to think how upset little Margie had been because the name of Stan's traveling companion had slipped out. She decided the man was probably one of those fishermen who didn't want any of their friends to know their favorite fishing spots for fear they'll be spoiled by crowds of campers.

She had heard Judge Bori holding forth on that very subject only the day before. He had his secret spots where the big ones lurked among the rocks of the little side streams. And he told nobody, but nobody, where they were!

She pulled into a service station at the other end of town. "Fill it up," she told the brisk attendant. "And have you a map that shows the road to Loon Lake?"

"Yes, Miss McCleod!" He grinned in recognition. And he not only filled the gas tank, wiped the windshield, and checked the tires but he got her autograph for his children's "Pioneer Days" souvenir book. "My kids think you're the prettiest queen we ever had," he told her. "They'll sure be tickled I had a chance to meet you!"

"Tell them hello for me!" Annette called as she drove away, feeling a warm glow toward a pleasant world. In just a couple of hours, she'd have the chance she had been hoping for—to help Stan's career.

The road that was marked by the gas station man was a well-kept dirt road, nicely surfaced for the first few miles, but rather narrow and steep. At first, it was dry, but as the car climbed up into the hills, she began to see reminders of the heavy storm that had visited the higher mountains a couple of days ago. There were puddles along the side of the road and some muddy stretches where torrents had cut across on their way down the sides of the mountains.

But the Monster performed like a champion and never once faltered as Annette drove higher into the more rugged Sierra country.

The air was becoming scented with pine, a sure sign that she was getting into high country. Although the trees along the sides of the road were slim and young, mere saplings, there were ancient forest giants nearby, huge trunks rising skyward a hundred or more feet.

Now and then, a stream would cascade down a broken granite slope so close to the road that Annette could feel the spray from it on her face as she drove by.

She checked her speedometer. She had only a few miles to go, if the map were accurate. It was time to start looking for road signs that the gasoline station man had told her should be there.

The road was winding around the side of a granite-strewn mountain whose head was in the clouds. One moment the road was in shadow, and the very next, she turned the shoulder of the mountain and found the sun blazing in her face. Dazzled by its brilliance for a moment, she failed to see the boulder lying on the outer edge of the slope directly in the Monster's path.

When Annette did see the boulder, she had only enough time to wrench her wheel over hard toward the inner side of the road to avoid hitting the chunk of granite. But the Monster's front and rear tires on that side sank deep into mud.

And though she used every bit of power that the little

car had under its hood, she couldn't get the Monster clear of the slippery trap.

"Well, here we sit, Monster, till somebody comes up the road and pulls us out!" But after a half hour of waiting, she realized that there might be very few people on this road that led only to a fishing lake. She might have to sit several hours before anyone came along, and Mr. Bradley of Astral Records would have crossed Stan Turner off his list long before they could get back to Lost Creek.

"Guess I'll have to start walking," Annette decided, and began the climb at a brisk pace. "When I get to the cabin, wherever it is, I'll get Stan's friend to bring his car and pull the Monster out of that mudhole. Then Stan and I can drive on down to Lost Creek, and after he's seen Mr. Bradley, I can drive him back up here again."

It was a cheerful little program with only one drawback. Loon Lake and the mountain that towered over it were still quite a distance ahead of her, and the hot sun soon slowed her down to a walk—a slow and weary walk by the time she had gone half a mile.

Annette was tired and thirsty, and her feet hurt. Finally, she spotted a road sign up ahead. She hurried on in spite of her discomfort, till she could read what it said: LOON

LAKE RESORT—2 MILES. Two *more* miles? The road that the sign pointed to was narrower than the one she had been traveling, and it wound up abruptly through a heavy stand of timber. But there were tire tracks on it, tracks of a heavy car or truck. And she could tell they had been made since the rain, because the weeds had been ground into the mud and hadn't sprung upright again.

"I bet it was Mr. Martin's car that left those tracks!" she told herself, pleasantly relieved to have even that much assurance that she was headed toward Stan.

But the sun was sinking down behind the farther peaks, and unless she hurried on, she might be caught by darkness before she found Stan. It was almost four o'clock already!

I could give it up and go home, thought Annette. I suppose by now Mr. Bradley has started back to the city. But maybe he'll wait around a little longer, if he really thinks anything of Stan's voice. I guess I'd better go on, she decided.

So Annette continued on as rapidly as her tired legs would take her. She hoped somebody in the resort could tell her where the Turner cabin was.

But when she came to the end of the two miles and saw the first old ramshackle structure that had been part of the

Loon Lake Resort, she knew that there wouldn't be much information available at that "resort." Its three broken-down shacks were roofless and showed only gaping holes where doors had been. Most of the wood that was removable had been carried off, probably by hunters.

So Annette went on again. And then, quite suddenly, she rounded a bend and came in sight of a pretty little lake, two hundred feet down in a cup of a valley.

The sun was setting in a riot of pink and purple, and the scurrying clouds high above the lake were reflected in its glasslike surface. Well, at last! she thought with relief. And now, where is that cabin?

She scanned the far slopes of the mountains that fringed the little lake, but the pines were so thick that all she could see was a mass of green.

It was silent, except for the birdcalls, and even those sounded sleepy. She was startled for a moment as a pair of quail took off from the brush and flew so close to her head that they almost touched it. She knew what they were up to. They undoubtedly had some chicks very near and were trying to distract the intruder's attention.

"No gun, just a flashlight!" she told the pair softly. "I'm not going to hurt your babies!" And it almost seemed as if they had understood, because the mother quail swept past again and settled down at the edge of the brush. She gave a soft, throaty call, and four tiny chicks came out of the weeds to her. Once they were all about her, she scuttled away with all four following in a straight line, and they disappeared in the underbrush.

Somewhere not very far away, a wildcat wailed like a banshee, and Annette hastily picked up a piece of pine branch from the roadside. It wasn't much of a weapon, but it might scare off the howler if Annette could remember to wave the stick and yell, "Shoo!" instead of taking to her heels. But the cat didn't cry again, and she soon got over her fright.

She went to the edge of the road and looked down the mountainside to the lake. No cabin, no plume of smoke rising above the tops of the trees. If Stan Turner and his friend had come to Loon Lake, as Margie had thought, they didn't seem to be around now.

Guess I'd better go on back to the car and hope that somebody comes along soon with a truck that can pull the Monster out of that mudhole, she thought. But she decided to sit down on a nearby rock and rest a few minutes first.

It was then that she heard the rustling in the brush. It was a louder rustling than any small animal would make. She could hear twigs snapping.

Annette jumped to her feet, staring around nervously, and gripping the pine branch again. If it were that wildcat, she'd be ready. Or perhaps it might be a bear. If it turned out to be a bear—well, then she'd forget about saying, "Shoo!" She'd just start running down the road and hope that he had enjoyed a good dinner and wouldn't feel like running after her!

But no hairy bulk came lumbering out of the dark tangle of underbrush, and there was no more rustling. Maybe it was some poor little deer hurrying home to his family, she thought, relieved.

The old prospector in the long white beard peered out at her from behind a giant pine tree. "By doggies, I near ran into that female! The mountain's gittin' plum crowded!" And he continued to watch her as she sat down on the rock and rested.

Twilight had set in now, and night would follow it swiftly, Annette knew. She had better be starting back to her car. She'd feel a lot safer in it, tucked under Aunt Lila's car robe, and a great deal warmer, along toward morning. She was glad her aunt had made her bring that robe with her to the Sierras!

She rose wearily and was about to start down the road again when her eyes fell on the far slope of the mountain and she saw a pinpoint of light among the pines. The cabin! She felt sure of it! And it couldn't be more than another half mile away on this very road.

Her weariness vanished as she started out briskly along the road, using her flashlight to guide her steps. By its light, she saw the impressions of the same heavy tire tracks she had noticed earlier at the turnoff. In the dazzle of the sunset, she hadn't seen them here before.

Before she had gone half the distance to the spot where the light shone among the trees, the full moon had risen and was flooding the landscape with pale silver. There was no need to use a flashlight. It was almost as bright as day.

Soon she reached the cabin in the center of a clearing. It was very small and old, and the door stood open.

The mellow rays of a kerosene lamp shone out through the doorway. That was the beacon she had seen from halfway around the lake. Smoke was rising from the stone chimney.

She hesitated at the edge of the clearing, listening to the

men's voices inside the cabin. She was too far away to make out their words, but one of the voices was loud and rough, and they both sounded angry.

After a moment, there was silence. Guess I'd better let them know they've got company, or I might hear some words I don't want to know, she thought. Then she started again toward the shack.

"Pssst! Pssst!" It came from close beside her and stopped her abruptly with visions of snakes. But when she turned to see what was hissing, it was only a skinny old-timer with a white beard.

He was motioning her back, and as he hurried out of the shadows on the edge of the clearing, she waited, surprised, to see what he wanted.

"Hold back there, missy. That's no place fer a lady!" he whispered loudly as he came up to her.

"But I have to see someone in there! At least, I think he's in there," she protested aloud.

Before she could say any more, he had clapped a bony hand across her mouth and pulled her back into the shadows with him. "Hush, yuh little idjut!" he scolded in an angry whisper. "They're comin' out!"

And as she pushed the old man's hand away from her

mouth and wrenched herself free to run toward the house, she saw Stan move past the lighted lamp in the cabin and start toward the door.

"There he is now!" she told the old man indignantly. But before she could take a step toward Stan or call to him, she heard the rough voice of the other man call out.

"And don't try to run off, because if you ain't back in here with that wood in just one minute, I'm coming after you. And this gun ain't no toy pistol!"

Annette stopped, gasping. The old man was at her side. "I told yuh! Just stay put or you'll wish yuh had!" And this time, she obeyed the order.

Stan went to the woodpile at the side of the cabin and picked up several chunks of firewood.

"Stealin' my wood, too, drat 'em!" the old man muttered. "Wisht I had me a gun! I'd drive them varmints outta my shack!" They watched Stan go back into the cabin.

"*Your* shack?" Annette was surprised.

"Been livin' there nigh onto ten years, barrin' a few trips to the Tuolumne for some diggin'. Been away this time around about a year, mebbe two years. Don't rightly remember how long." He frowned suddenly. "But it's still my shack, an' them claim jumpers got no right to move in!"

"But they're just vacationers, not claim jumpers, I'm sure! At least, Stan is. I don't know anything about Mr. Martin, except I don't think I like him."

"He's mean, that one. Bullies that young one, cuffs him around. I been watchin'." He stared at her, suspiciously, all of a sudden. "Come to think of it, missy, what's a young lady like you doin' up here lookin' for the likes of those two?"

"I had good news for Stan Turner. He's the young man in there." Annette was tired and worried.

"Stan Turner, you say? Well, that makes it different! If he's Stan Turner, that means he's my pardner Paul Turner's young'un! I've heard him talk about his son!"

It was Annette's turn to be mystified. "His father's name *is* Paul. What do you mean, he's your partner?"

"Jist what I say! Paul saved my life, fixed me up when that dad-ratted rattler bit me in the jaw. An' every claim I stake I put his name alongside mine! Someday we'll hit it big, me an' Paul! Got one that looks mighty promisin' right now! Figger I'll be driftin' down to Lost Creek one of these days to see Paul and give him the good news. Ain't seen him for a long time."

"He's in prison! For robbing *you*, if you're Joe

Robbins—and you must be! People think he killed you!"

"Sure am, sis! And what's this about killin' me?"

She told him the story as Stan Turner had told it to her. At the end, the old prospector looked grim.

"Reckon we'd better get ourselves down to Lost Creek tomorrow, sis, and straighten this mess out for Paul." He frowned. "You got an autymobile somewheres?"

"Stuck in a ditch back four miles," she answered glumly. Then she brightened. "But maybe if we told Stan and Mr. Martin all about it, they'd lend us Mr. Martin's car. We could bring it back by tomorrow night!" She was all ready to rush to the cabin, but he stopped her with a quick shake of the head.

"Hold on, little lady! That feller in there with a gun is holdin' that boy a prisoner from what I been hearing. He ain't gettin' his claws on me—or you! We'll git your car out of the mud somehow, first thing in the mornin'. Meantime, I've got grub at my camp. An' a safe place for you to rest the night."

"But wouldn't it be better—even if we have to steal Mr. Martin's car—to get down the mountain tonight?"

The old man shook his head. "Trouble is, he don't have

a car no more! He run it over the edge into the ravine this mornin'! I found what was left of it a few hours ago! Him an' Paul Turner's boy are stranded up here, and when we git back up with the law tomorrow night, we'll take him easy. I got a feelin' there's a price on his head!"

# 20      *The Threads Untangle*

"Do you suppose Annette could have meant it when she said she was eloping?" Tonia asked her mother anxiously. "I was sure she was joking, talking about a lion tamer!"

"Of course she was, silly! She's probably with Lola or one of the other girls, cooking up some surprise for the social tonight!" But Mrs. Bori was just guessing wildly so her own doubts wouldn't bother her so much. It wasn't like Annette to stay away without calling her family.

The doorbell rang, and Tonia ran to answer it. "That must be Annette now!"

But it was Johnny Abbott instead. He was dressed in his handsome costume as Prince Charming. "Hi, dreamboat!

You two queenies all set to dazzle the natives?" He swaggered in to show off his costume, complete with plumed hat and sword.

"Annette isn't here. And we haven't heard from her!" a worried Tonia told him.

"Hey! That reminds me!" Johnny frowned. "Pa's letting me use his car tonight, and when I took it to the filling station for a wash job this afternoon, the guy there told me Annette had asked him the way to Loon Lake this morning!"

"Loon Lake!" Judge Bori exclaimed from the library doorway. "Why would she go there?"

"Eloping?" Tonia suggested faintly.

"With whom, pray?" The judge scowled reprovingly.

"Uh!" Johnny was remembering something else.

"What is it?" Judge Bori asked, fixing him with a stare.

"Well, Stan Turner can't be located, either. A guy from Astral Records has been hanging around all day, waiting to get in touch with him. But nobody's seen him since yesterday." He gulped. "Maybe he and Annette—"

"I can't believe Annette would do anything so foolish!" Mrs. Bori wailed. "Oh, dear! Archie and Lila will blame us for not taking better care of her! This is dreadful!"

"Oh, Dad!" Tonia looked as if she were about to cry. "What are we going to do?"

"There's nothing *to* do!" Judge Bori said sternly. "I suggest that you two go on to the social and do not mention Annette's absence to anyone."

So Tonia and Johnny went and had a very good time as queen and consort. And to everyone who asked where Annette was, she gave the impression, without actually telling a fib, that Annette was still battling the headache that had kept her home the previous night.

But, secretly, Tonia was convinced that Annette and Stan had run away together, and she wished something romantic like that would happen to her. It would be thrilling!

The first rays of the Sierra sun were warming the mouth of the old mine shaft high on the hill above Loon Lake when Joe Robbins awoke.

All night, the aged prospector had kept watch over his sleeping guest as she lay rolled up in his blankets just inside the shaft entrance. He had no weapon except his pickax, but he was ready to use that on any intruder, man or beast. As dawn grayed the sky, he had dropped off to sleep, leaning against a rock, the pickax still clutched in his hand.

Now he rose and peered in at the sleeping girl. She had not moved. He tiptoed about, starting a cooking fire, and when it was ready, he began warming the beans and bacon that were his usual breakfast.

But it was the smell of coffee bubbling in the battered coffeepot that woke Annette. She staggered out, rubbing her eyes and shivering in the thin mountain air.

"There's a little spring behind the rocks over there if you crave to wash up, missy," Robbins informed her. "Then we'll eat fast an' git on our way down to your autymobile."

The spring water was ice-cold, but refreshing, as she splashed it on her face, and her cheeks were glowing when she dried them with her handkerchief. She was starting back to the campfire when she heard the voices of the men at the cabin down the mountain. They came clearly to her. She listened, startled.

"Come back here, or I'll shoot!" she heard the rough voice command angrily. "Looks like I'll have to tie you up!"

"I was just looking around. Thought I'd go catch some fish." That was Stan's voice.

"Get inside here!" the other voice ordered, and Annette

heard no more, though she waited tensely a couple of minutes. Then she ran back to Joe Robbins to tell him.

"We better eat quick an' get that car out of the mud," Robbins told her. "Sooner we git to Lost Creek and back with help for that Turner boy, the better for him! No tellin' what that cuss'll do if the lad riles him!"

So they ate quickly and were soon on their way down to the car. The burros went willingly. They were always willing to trot a downhill trail.

But it was almost four miles to where Annette's sports car had bogged down in the mudhole, and long before they covered half the distance, both Annette and the burros had slowed to a walk.

At the Bori home in Lost Creek, breakfast was a quiet meal. They were waiting anxiously for word from Annette.

Tonia was still secretly thrilled at the thought of Annette having eloped so romantically, but she kept it to herself. Her parents were amazed that sensible Annette could have done such a foolish thing. No one felt like talking.

Then they heard the doorbell ring several times.

Katey scurried to answer it, hopefully, but it wasn't the telegram they all expected.

It was a woman demanding to talk to Judge Bori or his wife at once. She seemed in a desperate hurry.

They could hear Katey telling her that the judge and Mrs. Bori were at breakfast and couldn't be disturbed.

The woman's voice came sharply: "But it's about his niece! She may be in terrible danger!"

Judge Bori almost knocked his chair over as he rose and strode to the door. "Mrs. Turner!" He was amazed to see the wife of the man whom he had sentenced to prison two years ago. "What's this about Annette?"

"Judge! You've got to do something right away!" She was almost hysterical as the judge drew her inside the hallway and sent Katey away.

Tonia and her mother hurried to join them and stood by, shocked, as Mrs. Turner told about the escaped convict who had stolen a car and forced Stan to drive him up to Loon Lake. "He said he'd kill Stan if I sent the police after them, so I didn't dare tell anyone! But my little girl didn't know what was going on, and she told your niece where to find Stan. She's probably up there now, and maybe a prisoner of that terrible man—"

"I'll call Police Chief Trujillo at once! He'll get his men together and go after them!"

"Warn him to be careful!" Mrs. Turner pleaded. "Don't let Martin see them coming, or he might kill both Stan and your niece!"

Not more than ten minutes later, a squad of grim-faced men, armed with rifles and side arms, left Lost Creek in a fast car headed up toward Loon Lake.

Chief Trujillo had checked his records for the name of Jim Martin and found that he was a dangerous escaped convict from State Prison. He had a long record of serious crimes and might stop at nothing to stay free.

Up at the old shack, Stan sat on the edge of the bunk with his hands tied behind him, watching Martin make up a bundle of food and supplies and wrap it in a blanket.

Martin was feeling talkative. "First car that comes along, either direction, I'll come limpin' out of the bushes with a sob story about losin' my horse. And when they pick me up, I'll show 'em this little persuader!" He tapped the revolver in his belt and laughed coarsely.

When the bundle was securely tied, he swung it onto his shoulder and moved toward the door. "I left you some slack in that rope," he said to Stan, with a nasty grin. "You can wiggle free in a coupla hours, if you try!"

Stan glared at him and made an effort to free his wrists, but the rope was too tight. Martin laughed. "So long, kid! Hope you git loose before the bears come snoopin' for those scraps on the table!" He was still laughing as he went out, leaving the door wide open.

Stan staggered to his feet and looked around desperately for some means of freeing his wrists. But even the little kerosene lamp that they had brought from the house was useless. The convict had taken all the matches.

Stan had no intention of staying there for the bears. He staggered out and started down the road, his hands still tied. He had no idea what he could do to stop Jim Martin from finding another victim, but he had to try. A warning yell, anything, might help!

Far down the road, Annette and old Joe Robbins had reached the mired Monster.

"Tain't as bad as I figgered it might be," the old prospector told Annette after inspecting the situation. "Chico and Brownie can haul the fool thing clear in no time!" And he tied ropes to the Monster's bumper and rigged up a yoke for the two burros.

But the little sports car only settled deeper into the mud, and very soon the burros got tired of pulling and refused to move. Joe Robbins coaxed and cajoled them in vain. It was only when Annette picked a couple of handfuls of lush green grass and wildflowers and held them temptingly before the two twitching noses that the burros condescended to do some more hauling in an effort to get at the tasty stuff.

At last—with a squishy *plop*—the Monster left its muddy bed and crawled slowly up onto the dry road behind the munching burros. Annette ran around and got into the driver's seat. Hope it runs, she thought, turning on the ignition. And after a moment of suspense, some protesting groans, a shiver or two, and a couple of barks, the Monster came roaring to life. "Hooray, we did it!" Annette crowed. "Thanks, Chico and Brownie!"

Old Joe Robbins freed his burros, who were showing signs of wanting to kick the frightening object that was making threatening roars at them. They scampered off into the brush. "Let 'em go. I can find 'em again. They won't go far!" he told her.

Annette drove up the road to a spot that was wide enough and made a careful turnabout.

But just as she was about to start down again, a black-bearded man came into view, running down the road and calling to her, "Hey! How about a lift, lady?"

She was so startled that she stopped—and killed the motor. The voice was that of the rough-spoken man who had been holding Stan Turner prisoner!

She started the motor again, but by that time the bearded man had reached the side of the car and pulled open the door. He was holding a gun in his hand as he ordered, "Keep movin', miss, and you won't git hurt!"

Joe had recognized him the moment he had come into sight. Yelling and flourishing his pickax, he ran to the middle of the road. "Stop! Look out, missy—it's him!"

A bullet whistled past old Robbins's head, and he jumped back out of the way. The car went by, but not far. Annette drove it deliberately into the same mudhole in which it had rested all night! And there it landed, jolting both Annette and the swearing Martin, and throwing the convict against the windshield.

His revolver was jarred out of his hand and dropped out of the car into the deep mud puddle.

By the time he had scrambled out of the car and was trying to fish it up, the car full of Chief Trujillo's deputies

had come roaring up the road and the men were piling out with drawn guns.

And it was while the deputies were marching their prisoner back to the police car in handcuffs that Chief Trujillo took a good look at the bewhiskered old man who was dancing up and down in glee at the happy outcome.

"Joe Robbins!" He stared in utter amazement. "Thought you were dead and gone!"

"Well, I ain't! An' you better let Paul Turner out o' prison right off! Him an' me have some gold claims to work—rich ones!" He laughed gleefully.

Chief Trujillo was still a little stunned, but he was getting over it fast. He turned on Jim Martin. "Where's the Turner boy?" he demanded. "What did you do with him?"

"Dunno what you're talkin' about!" The convict leered.

But just then Stan Turner came into sight, staggering down the road with his hands still tied behind him.

"Stan!" Annette ran toward him. "You're all right!"

He was amazed to see them all—and delighted when he saw old Joe Robbins, the man he had been searching for with unshaken faith.

It was a triumphant procession back to Lost Creek, and once the whole story was told, Annette and Stan were both on the front pages of the local and city newspapers.

And it was a great help to Stan's career. Even though Mr. Bradley had given up and gone back to the city when Stan had failed to contact him, he came back again the next morning, a contract in one pocket and a copy of the morning paper in the other.

"Local Boy a Smash Hit on Record!" the *Gazette* boasted a few weeks later. And they gave the story of his success more space than the committee's "Report on Profits from the Pioneer Days Celebration"!

That morning, Annette, packing to go home after her Sierra vacation, found a copy of Stan's first record in her mail, and she and Tonia called the gang in to hear it. They thought it was great! Even Johnny admitted that it wasn't bad—for a first.

There had been a note with the record, but she had tucked it away in the secret compartment of her wallet after reading it a dozen times. It was a very nice, private note, and it thanked her for all she had done to help him and his family.

She knew it by heart. And as she drove the Monster down the road to home, she thought of what he had written: "The city's fine, but lonesome. Hope you'll like my first album. It's to be called *Songs for Annette*." And then, at the bottom of the page: "I'll be making a personal appearance in your town next month. Hope you'll find time to let me see you."

"That," she said, smiling at herself in the rearview mirror above her windshield, "I certainly will!"